FAMILY TIES

WITH DARK DEVILS SERIES PREQUEL

SAVAGELY DEPRAVED

J.L. QUICK

COPYRIGHT

TRIGGER WARNINGS

This novel contains content that might be triggering for some readers, they are the Devils of Adelaide Cove after all.

Your mental health is important.

Please review the content warnings at the link below.

MEET THE DEVILS OF ADELAIDE COVE

"Hell is empty and all the devils are here."

—**William Shakespeare, The Tempest**

Adelaide Cove

Case # 4395-D87-473

Adelaide Cove Police De

CASE #

439

PORT DATE	INCIDENT DATE	REP(
8/13/2021	ongoing	

ME/ALL KNOWN ALIASES

Geyer, Grant

YSICAL DESCRIPTION/IDENTIFIABLE MARKS

6'1". Roughly 210 lbs, 44 years old, Caucasian, Grey Hair,

3 roses tattooed on his right pec

OWN FACTS

Software Security Engineer (runs mutli-billion dollar company

Geyer Software from his home). Son: Garrison Geyer

URED/DECEASED

Stephanie Geyer (Spouse) - Drown in residential pool (7/2007),

cause of death deemed suspicious, Madeline O'Rourk (8/2019)

Victoria Mews (Housekeeper) - Missing since 12/2020

TES

Speculation regarding Mr. Geyer's captivity of Ms. Mews remains

unfounded at this time

PROVED BY	FORWARD TO
Det. David Michales	

NATURE

CA:

4.

ORT DATE	INCIDENT DATE	REP
3/13/2021	ongoing	

ME/ALL KNOWN ALIASES

Parker, Edmund

YSICAL DESCRIPTION/IDENTIFIABLE MARKS

6'2", Roughly 220 lbs, 40years old, Caucasian, Brown Hair, green

eyes

OWN FACTS

Real Estate Investor, owns most of Adelaide Cove and new

housing developments in surrounding communities

URED/DECEASED

Paisley Allen (11/2021), Brittney Jones (4/2022), Lisa Tolinger

5/2022), Elise Allen (10/2022), Liv Alden (7/2023)

TES

Women seen with Mr. Parker within months of their disappearance,

o confirmed leads.

Psychiatric profile: sexual sadist

PROVED BY	FORWARD TO
Det. David Michales	

NATURE

Adelaide Cove Polic...

PORT DATE	INCIDENT DATE
8/13/2021	ongoing

ME/ALL KNOWN ALIASES

Cattaneo, William

YSICAL DESCRIPTION/IDENTIFIABLE MARKS

6'2", Roughly 220 lbs, 43years old, Caucasian, Brown/Greying hair, hazel eyes, see attached for identifiable marks

OWN FACTS

Restaurateur, moved to Adelaide Cove 8/2019

URED/DECEASED

Cameryn Weathers (8/2021)

TES

Unable to locate any information regarding suspect prior him moving to Adelaide Cove

PROVED BY	FORWARD TO
Det. David Michales	

NATURE

Adelaide Cove Police Department

CASE 4.

REPORT DATE	INCIDENT DATE	REP
8/13/2021	ongoing	

NAME/ALL KNOWN ALIASES

Beaufort, Elizabeth

PHYSICAL DESCRIPTION/IDENTIFIABLE MARKS

5'6"", Roughly 125 lbs, 32years old, Caucasian, Brown Hair, Blue Eyes

KNOWN FACTS

Widower, socialite

INJURED/DECEASED

Benedict Beaufort (Spouse) 10/2013, natural causes (age 78)

NOTES

connected to Grant Geyer, Edmund Parker, and William Cattaneo, Madeline O'Rourk (8/2019), Cameryn Weathers (8/2021), Paisley Allen (11/2021), suspected ties to sex ring

APPROVED BY	FORWARD TO
Det. David Michales	

SIGNATURE

Adelaide Cove

473

PORT DATE	INCIDENT DATE
3/13/2021	ongoing

NAME/ALL KNOWN ALIASES

Millington, Samuel

PHYSICAL DESCRIPTION/IDENTIFIABLE MARKS

5'4" Roughly 235 lbs, 32 years old, Caucasian, Brown Hair, Brown Eyes

KNOWN FACTS

Retired NFL player

INJURED/DECEASED

Joseph Ruark - Assault (5/2018), Chloe Wilson (8/2019), Mia Dillon (9/2022 - filed assault charge and left town)

NOTES

Seen with Grant Geyer, Edmund Parker, William Cattaneo, and Elizabeth Beaufort. Recanted sexual assault claim 2016.

APPROVED BY	FORWARD TO
Det. David Michales	

SIGNATURE

Dark
DEVILS

THE SAVAGELY DEPRAVED SERIES

DARK DEVILS

To everyone seeking an irredeemable,

morally-black billionaire

as their next book boyfriend

(or girlfriend),

this one's for you...

CHAPTER ONE

EDMUND

Noting the time, I close the lid of my laptop and throw on my suit jacket. The lights flicker on automatically as I step into the garage. My fingers linger over the sets of keys neatly hung by the door, before settling on the Bentley Bacalar. Pushing the ignition, I pull from the garage the moment the door rises.

Being late for Inauguration Night would be in poor taste.

Forgoing posted speed limits through town, I make my way toward the sprawling estates located along the wooded outskirts. I travel the dark, desolate, winding roads at excessive speeds, only slowing when I approach the destination. Stopping before a tall, ornate iron gate I pull my access card from the breast pocket of my jacket and swipe it over the sensor of the modified call box.

I shift the car back into drive as the large gate swings slowly open to provide me entry. Pulling through, I pause to ensure they close behind me. Once I am satisfied, my foot stomps on the accelerator and I swiftly make my way up the long, tree-line private road.

Passing through the trees and into the massive clearing, I turn onto the half circle driveway before pulling to a stop. Noting the cars beside me, I am quite certain that Grant, Will and Liz are already inside with The Kid.

Stepping from the car, I walk toward the elaborate estate. From the outside it looks like any of the other well-concealed, multi-million-dollar homes surrounding Adelaide Cove, but inside it's our playground.

As early as my teen years, I learned that my sexual interests were not...vanilla.

Bending the head cheerleader over a balcony? Snooze.

Knowing her jock boyfriend was just below us as I slid my cock into her? Boring.

Digging my fingers into her hips deep enough for blood to pool beneath my nails and fucking her so hard she struggled not to squeal? Better...

Exploring my desires, I was repeatedly labeled as savage, dark, depraved...

Sadistic.

None of which are lies.

There isn't exactly an abundance of women willing to toy with the possibility of death just to please their partner. And that is how I wound up here—at the home of the Savagely Depraved.

As we like to call it.

Taking the stairs to the front entrance door, it opens for me when I reach the landing. Beside the door stands a well-dressed man holding a tray containing my drink—a Classic Manhattan with an orange twist. Silently, he dips his head while extending the tray in my direction.

Drink in hand, the sound of my leather-soled shoes on the marble floor echoes throughout the grand foyer as I make my way to the study at the rear of the home. Sitting around the room are the others—Grant, Liz, Will, and The Kid.

Who eventually I'll probably need to stop calling him The Kid.

Like me, they all harbor a darkness they aren't willing to pretend doesn't exist just because it doesn't meet societal expectations of what is considered a 'normal' sexual proclivity.

Grant, the IT security expert, who could probably wipe the Queen of England from digital existence if he so pleased. A skill that comes in handy when you like to ensure your woman of choice is tied up at your beck-and-call twenty four seven. Literally tied up and available.

William, the mysterious billionaire without a past – or at least not one that most people will ever know of. As one of the few with some insight as to his life before Adelaide Cove, it makes sense that the man enjoys a good hunt on the property on occasion.

His gorgeous girlfriend, Elizabeth, who I playfully refer to as the gold-digging whore. She, herself, will admit that she didn't exactly marry her late husband, Benedict, for love. This gorgeous woman is our queen—more correctly, our cuckquean. She is also our madam, and procurer of women more than eager to allow us to indulge in our fantasies—for a price.

And lastly, The Kid, Samuel—a recently retired NFL player, who doesn't always require that his women to be willing participants when tending to his needs. In lieu of a screaming partner, he'll take the look of terror that comes with asphyxiation.

But who wouldn't?

Taking a seat next to Liz, I throw my arm around her shoulder and place a kiss on her cheek before whispering in her ear, "You look fucking stunning tonight."

CHAPTER TWO

ELIZABETH

"We've talked about this, Eddie," my voice soft and sultry as I lean into him and use the nickname I know he hates. "I have no interest in being one of your little whipping posts for the night. The only way your cock is going anywhere near me is if you give me the extreme pleasure of watching you and Will first."

"And I have no interest in fucking or being fucked by Edmund," William chimes in from the chair across from us.

"Too bad," I raise a brow and flick my finger under Edmund's chin before standing from the couch.

Eventually, they'll come around.

"Okay boys," I address the men in the room, "tonight's buy-in is two-million-dollars."

Without hesitating, they all pull their phones from their

pockets and make the necessary offshore bank transfers to fund their entertainment for the evening.

Sure, any drug-addicted whore working downtown will give you five minutes in an alley for fifty to hundred dollars, but good pussy doesn't come cheap.

And when you have the interests of these men, you pay extra. A lot extra if you plan to cause permanent damage.

The girls that I procure are grad students and business professionals. Each of them looks as though they just stepped from a gentleman's magazine, having toned bodies and perky tits that even make me jealous.

After being vetted, and receiving a thorough health exam, they sign a non-disclosure and a contract for one night of whatever we please. In exchange, they receive a million-dollar payout.

What they do after tonight...

More of them should probably walk away with their money at the end of the night, instead of making the mistake of getting entangled with anyone in this room long-term.

"Can you handle that, Kid," Edmund shoots a glance at Samuel. "Or do you need to call your mommy and daddy to ask for money first."

"At what point do we drop this Kid stuff?" Samuel questions while shoving his phone back into his pocket.

"Maybe after you prove that you deserve to be here," Edmund smirks at him, "that you actually fit in with the rest of us."

"If you boys are done measuring your cocks," I shoot them both an annoyed glance, "I'd like to introduce you to the ladies."

The four of them rise from their seats without delay, and follow behind me as we make our way to the sitting room where tonight's women are waiting.

They might enjoy a cock measuring contest from time to time, but everyone here knows that mine, although symbolic, is by far the biggest.

"You're awfully quiet tonight, Grant," I slip my arm into his as we all make our way to the East wing. "Not quite up for tonight's festivities?"

"Sweet child," his deep, mature voice practically melts my panties. "Don't let the graying hair and fine lines fool you. I am always up for festivities, as you call them. I'll happily show you just how up for them I am when you're ready to get rid of *you know who.*"

"Mr. Geyer," I gasp, pretending to clutch my pearls. "What kind of woman do you think I am?"

"If only I could chain you up," he smirks, "you just might be the perfect kind."

These men are obnoxious flirts, and I love it. But we all know that I'm not going to give into their desires, just like most of them are not going to give in to mine—with the exception of Will.

He is more than willing to be my hot husband, degrading and denying me as I watch him with other women until he's ready for me to join. In exchange, I submit to his primal and animalistic desires.

"Gentlemen," I pull open the door to the sitting room and the four women promptly stand as we step inside. I gesture to them, "The ladies for this evening – Madeline, Paisley, Cameryn, and Chloe."

The women, all in their twenties, are dressed in sleek, black cocktail dresses with matching stilettos. Beneath their evening attire, each is wearing varying versions of expensive black lingerie. They vary slightly in appearance, but each of them is beautiful and looks as though she has the presence and stature to belong in our world.

"Samuel," I gesture to the women before us. "As the man of honor this evening, you get first pick."

CHAPTER THREE

SAMUEL

Taking my time, I walk toward them. My eyes gaze over the four women, each of them absolutely fucking beautiful.

Madeline is a tall, curvaceous brunette. A little too curvy for my taste with her obviously fake tits. Without giving her so much as a second glance, I continue down the row to Paisley.

Her long, wavy dirty-blonde hair cascades over her shoulders, shrouding her physique. Sliding my hand over her shoulder, I provide us all with a better view of the natural curves it was hiding. My fingers trail down her spine, lingering at the curvature of her ass as my other hand dusts along the outer curve of her breast. She stands tall, confident, and unwavering.

Slowly pulling my hands from her, I place one on Cameryn's hip. The stamina that likely couples her athletic build intrigues me, the similarities her facial features share with my sister much less so.

Apparently, we all have our limits.

Chloe's eyes are fixated at the floor as I approach. She is a petite redhead with porcelain skin that will show every mark my fingers leave around her throat. A tad less curvy than I prefer, but of the four of them, she is obviously the most hesitant about her decision to join us for the evening. Slipping my finger under her chin, I tip her face up to meet my dark gaze. She struggles to maintain eye contact with me, trepidatious fear already coursing through her veins.

Bending down, I place a chaste kiss on her lips. While brief, I can feel them tremble against mine.

"I'll take Chloe," I announce to the others, and turn to find Liz extending her fist to the other three men.

"As always, long straw goes first, and short straw goes last." She waits for each of the men to pull one of the small wooden dowels from her hand. When she's gone down the line, she gestures for them all to present them. A slight smirk ticks at the corner of her lips when she notices that Will has the next choice of the women.

He steps close to Liz, pulls her flush against him, and places a deep kiss against her lips. Pulling back, he stares into her eyes as his deep voice billows throughout the room, "You pick, baby girl. Which one of these beautiful women do you want to watch me fuck tonight?"

"Do I get to join?" she whispers with a flirtatious tone.

"Yes," he pauses. "If you pick well. Pick poorly and you will be going home dripping and unsatisfied this evening."

Her eyes light up at his words, and he gently releases his tight embrace on her. She confidently crosses the room to the three remaining women and stands before them.

"You have a gorgeous fucking body," Liz slides her hand down Madeline's side. "It's too bad you're brunette. I don't want him thinking about me when he fucks you."

Liz places a soft kiss at the corner of Madeline's mouth before placing herself in front of Paisley and Cameryn. Her thumbs rub over each of their lower lips before commanding, "Open your mouths."

They both willfully comply, and she slides two fingers over each of their tongues. "Suck," her words confident and domineering. "Show me how good you'll be at sucking my Will's fat cock."

I watch intently as the two women take Liz's fingers to the backs of their throats. Both slide their mouths over the length of her fingers, eagerly continuing to swallow her to the knuckle. Both are obviously quite skilled in their ability to suck a cock, but it's Cameryn's unwavering stare into Liz's eyes that causes my cock to twitch.

"Good girls," Liz slides her fingers from their mouths, using the bottom of Paisley's dress to dry them.

"Cameryn," Liz smiles at Will, and he looks equally content with her choice.

"Paisley," Edmund quickly makes his choice before stepping to the two remaining women. He firmly grips her chin and yanks her face up to his, "So fucking pretty and confident...I'm going to enjoy breaking you."

"Grant, that leaves you with Madeline," Liz gestures between the two of them.

"I will happily take her," a devilish smile spreads across his face. "She reminds me of my beloved, Stephanie."

CHAPTER FOUR

GRANT

Crossing the room, I place my hand on the small of Madeline's back as the others retrieve their selected companions as well.

"Eddie," Liz's voice is firm yet condescending. "Maybe see to it that we don't have any repeats of last time. I have things to do tomorrow and would much prefer not to spend my evening cleaning up your mess."

*In Edmund's defense, he **had** told that girl to ensure she laid very still...*

"Come, my dear," my hand gently pushes against Madeline's back as I lead her out of the study and into the great room of the house.

The devil's playground.

This spacious room is filled with more than enough toys to keep all our deviant interests satisfied. Continuing to guide her through the room, I walk her toward my favorite section of playthings.

"Tell me, my dear," my fingers dance over the various options before me. "Have you been tied up before?"

"Yes," her voice is so soft that I that struggle to hear her as I pull her hands in front of her. Holding them in front of her stomach, she waits patiently with them facing palm up.

"And what kind of bindings have you been in before? Or found to be most enjoyable? Silk? Cotton? Hemp? Jute?" I pause between each type of rope, placing them in her hand to familiarize her with their feel.

"I have only known the smoothness of silk around my wrists, but I think I like the softness of the hemp," she hesitates for a moment, "Of course, use what you like."

"I intend to," my tone is flat as I grab a twenty-foot section of black jute with a tight lay. Placing it on the table beside me, I slowly turn Madeline. I sweep her chestnut brown hair over her shoulder and slowly undo the now exposed zipper running down the back of her dress. Slipping it from her shoulders, it slides down her body until it is pooled on the floor around her black stilettos, and I whisper into her ear, "You won't be needing this anymore this evening."

The body she was hiding beneath is perfect. She carries the same build as Stephanie, right down to the dimples in her lower back. My fingers linger over her skin as I turn her back to face me.

"Hands," I command, and she outstretches both of them to me. Doubling over the jute, I wrap it around her right wrist, cinch it tight and tie a knot. Keeping some slack, I repeat a similar cuff around her left wrist, leaving her wrists bound with several inches of rope between them.

She's going to be fucking gorgeous when she is bound and defenseless...

"Turn around," she tentatively turns on her heels until her back is facing me. My hands roam from her hips and up her sides before traveling down each of her arms to her bound wrists. Gingerly lifting them to her face, I whisper in her ear, "Now open your mouth, dear."

Gathering her hair in my hand, I twist the length of it down her spine. Pulling her wrists to the sides of her face, the slack of the jute that joins her wrists slides between her open lips. Tying a hitch knot at the nape of her neck, she winces when the jute suddenly becomes a tight gag. Holding the remainder of the rope, I braid it through her hair and secure it at the ends.

"Fuck," my lips growl against her neck, and my palm rubs over her ass as I walk her before the display of anal plugs and toys. "I can't decide if I want to add a hook or keep that tight little hole available for my cock."

Her eyes visibly widen when I lift a decent sized, stainless-steel plug and slather a generous amount of lubricant onto it.

"I need one big enough to stretch you out for my cock," I hook my fingers under the lace of her thong to provide me the access I need. "Bend over and relax."

Holding the tip against her ass, I press lightly as my free hand rubs against her lace-covered cunt. Twisting the plug slowly, I delicately work more of it inside of her. She moans as I repeatedly withdraw it and press it back into her. Her thighs quiver when I press the entirety of it into her, leaving the red jewel peeking around the lace of her thong between her pert ass cheeks.

Drool dribbles from her mouth and down her chin as she stands, the gag making it difficult for her to swallow.

"Allow me," Edmund steps next to her, cups her face and savors it as he licks it from her chin before turning his attention to me, "I'm not opposed to sharing these two this evening."

"As much as I'd enjoy watching Paisley eat her cunt, maybe next time. I have something special in store for this one."

Based on the O-ring gag, aggressive nipple clamps, and chained flogger he has before him, I'm pretty sure we would ruin his plans as well.

"I should've asked before the gag," I lead Madeline outside to the pool and smirk as I kneel before her and remove her shoes, "but how well can you hold your breath?"

CHAPTER FIVE

EDMUND

"Undress." My demanding tone startles Paisley and causes her to involuntarily jump.

Oh sweetheart, you have no idea how afraid you should actually be...

Wasting no time, she pulls the zipper on her dress and lets it fall from her body. She stands before me in a lacy bra, so sheer that I can see her pert nipples pressing into the fabric, matching panties, a garter and thigh highs.

Fucking exquisite.

"Bra too." My fingers flick against the pink flesh pressing into the lace and a quiet, pained groan falls from her lips. Unhooking the bra, she drops it to the floor to join her dress.

Roughly, I grab her breasts with both hands and knead them, pausing only to occasionally pinch her nipples. Replacing one of my hands with my mouth, I take her into my mouth and flick her nipple with my tongue. Sucking hard, I slowly slide my mouth from her until only her tight nipple is in my mouth. Biting down on the sensitive bundle of nerves, I roll it between my teeth. She trembles against my mouth, forced to endure my teeth for fear of the pain she'll submit herself to from trying to pull away.

As I relax my hold, my teeth graze her flesh as I slide her nipple from my mouth. The former pink flesh already showing signs of bruising.

A groan from the other side of the room draws her attention. Following her gaze, I find Cameryn still fully dressed on her knees. Her upper body rocking at a steady rhythm as she repeatedly takes Will's cock into her mouth.

Abruptly turning Paisley so that she is facing them, I pull her back against my chest. I toy with her sensitive nipple and slide my other hand beneath the lace of her panties. Rubbing my fingers over her pussy, I groan into her ear, "Does my little pain slut like to watch?"

At the same time as I roll her nipple between my fingers, I firmly rub the pads of my fingers over her hardened clit. Squirming against me, she quietly moans, "Yes."

"And what is it you enjoy?" I work my fingers faster, bringing her closer to the edge. "Watching her suck him off?"

"Yes." I feel the heat of embarrassment creep over her cheek against my face. Her hips arch against my hand and her breaths become raspy, my fingers rubbing her to the brink of her orgasm.

"Would you enjoy getting fucked while you watch them?" I roll her clit gently while waiting for her response, the one I already know the answer to.

"Please," she whimpers, both the answer to my question and her neediness to come. Rubbing over her clit, I feel her body tighten, her orgasm just seconds away. Promptly sliding my fingers from her panties, I wipe her arousal over her stomach.

"I don't feel like sharing tonight," I whisper in her ear before deepening my voice. "And they won't really enjoy what I have planned for you."

Keeping her back flush against my chest, I lift the butterfly clips from the table and dangle them before her face, "Do you know how these work?"

She shakes her head and I affix the clamp to her tender nipple, causing her to wince. The second only causes her breath to momentarily hitch.

"And to think, that's not even the good part," I release the chain connecting them and let it fall against her skin as I gather my other items from the table. Gripping the chain, a smirk creeps over my face as I give the faintest of tugs, "They get tighter when I pull."

A mewl quivers over her lips as they notch and tighten, and the sound of her pain travels straight to my cock.

"You might want to keep up," I begin walking from the room, holding tightly onto the chain as I force her to walk behind me.

Pained moans rattle from her as she struggles to maintain my brisk pace in her stilettos.

Fuck...

I need more of her moans.

And I'm dying to know what her screams sound like.

CHAPTER SIX

WILLIAM

"You fucking sit there, baby girl, and watch her suck my cock. Do you think she sucks better than you?"

Sliding my fingers into Cameryn's hair, I let her continue to set the pace. I usually like to be in charge, but she's a fucking pro at giving head. She works every inch of my length with her hands and mouth, while ensuring my balls also get a good bit of attention.

"She's so fucking eager," I toy with her nipple through her dress while I continue to tease Liz, "I bet she's wet and just as eager to take my cock."

Looking down at Cameryn, I'm met with her eyes staring up at me. Her head gently nodding in agreement as she continues to swallow me down her warm throat without missing a beat.

Sliding my cock from her mouth, I help Cameryn to her feet before turning my attention back to Liz, "Undress her for me. I want her in nothing but a garter and stockings. I want you to see how fucking soaked she is for me."

I work the buttons of my shirt while Liz follows my commands and undresses Cameryn. By the time she's in nothing but her garter and thigh highs, I've stripped off the remainder of my clothes.

Liz returns to her seat as I step toward Cameryn, effortlessly slipping a finger into her cunt before pulling out; my digit covered with her arousal. Pressing my slick finger into her mouth, she sucks it with the same eagerness as my cock.

"Such an eager little cock whore," I smile at her as I guide her back to her knees. Replacing my finger with my cock, she doesn't hesitate to begin swallowing me down her throat once again.

Watching Cameryn continue to suck me like a fucking champ, my eyes repeatedly glance at Liz. She fidgets in her seat, trying to qualm her neediness.

"Part those thighs for me," I stroke the hair from Cameryn's face. "Show her how you're fucking dripping for my cock."

Shifting her weight, she spreads her knees apart and places her glistening cunt and wet upper thighs on display.

"Play with that needy cunt while you suck my cock," I pull one of her hands from me and she immediately begins working her fingers over her clit.

"Hands on the chair, baby girl," I lightly fist Cameryn's hair as I address Liz. "You get to watch her come. You don't get to come unless I decide to let you."

Cameryn rubs at her clit with a fervent need, and she moans around my cock deep in her throat as she makes herself come.

"Fuck." I snarl while using my grip in her hair to roughly pull her from my cock. Spittle rolls down her chin and she stares up at me with a lustful and proud gaze as she makes her way to her feet.

"Straddle her lap," I gesture toward Liz. Cameryn struts the few steps to her, her pert ass swaying with each step, and places her knees on the cushion next to Liz's thighs. Stepping behind Cameryn, I snake my arm around her chest and pull her back to my chest as I straddle Liz's knees.

"Sit back, baby girl, watch as I slide my fat fucking cock into her cunt." My eyes are fixated on Liz as I press my tip inside of Cameryn. I groan as I slowly press the whole of me inside her, both from how tight she is and watching Liz chew at her lower lip with envy.

"Are you jealous? Do you have any idea how fucking tight her cunt is?" I sneer at Liz, "Because it feels like I barely fucking fit inside her."

Holding Cameryn in place, I repeatedly thrust into her hard and fast. Squeals of pleasure repeatedly rise from her lungs as I drive into her hard enough that her tits bounce in Liz's face.

"I'm going to make her come all over your fucking lap."
My hips work faster, and I struggle to get out the breathy
words. "I'm going to let her drip all over you before I leave
you wanting."

Cameryn clenches around my cock, screaming as she
comes, before crumpling against Liz.

"She's already fucking spent," I wrap my arms around
Cameryn and pull her from Liz. "And I'd still rather fuck
her tight cunt than yours."

CHAPTER SEVEN

EDMUND

"Hands on the wall and spread your legs," I growl, while shoving her face into the hallway wall. "I'd listen, because this is your only opportunity to come tonight before I use your holes solely for my pleasure."

Spreading her arms and legs, she stands like an 'X' with her hands on the wall, and I press two fingers deep into her cunt. Curling them, I work hard and fast until she is panting, and her knees are shaking.

"Do you think you deserve to come?" My tone dark and devilish as I pull my fingers from her, denying her the orgasm she was so close to.

"Only if you think I do," she trembles against the wall.

"Fuck, sweetheart," I whisper into her ear while grinding my cock against her, "Make it through this, you just might get an offer to make this a long-term arrangement. Would you like that?"

Without giving her an opportunity to answer, I press my fingers back into her slick channel and whisper into her ear, "Do you want to come on my fingers or my cock? For that comment, you deserve to come."

"Whatever you prefer." She arches her back and presses her hips toward me.

Fuck, every now and then one of these women surprises me.

"This time you get my fingers." I plunge two digits into her before slowly drawing them out. "If there's a next time, I might give you the honor of my cock."

"I look forward to your cock," she clenches around the fingers working roughly in her. "I'll happily come on your hand."

"Prove it." I add a third finger and thrust into her at a violent and relentless speed. Screaming as her fingers claw at the wall, her arousal runs down my arm and she comes hard on my hand.

"On your knees," I give a slight tug at the chain between her tits without giving her a chance to come down from her orgasm, and she drops to the floor. "And open your fucking mouth."

Pressing the O-ring gag to her lips, she opens wider to spread her lips around it. With her mouth gaping wide around the silicone ring, I buckle it behind her head.

"Just so you know," I drag the chain flogger over her ass. "I don't give a fuck if you take enjoyment from what happens next."

She stares up at me with wide eyes as I unzip my pants and pull out my throbbing cock. Fisting it before her face, my dark eyes stare into hers as I gravelly say, "I'm going to have my way with your face as I leave beautiful marks all over that ass of yours. And you're going to fucking take it until I spill every last drop of cum down that waiting throat of yours."

Spittle pools at her lips from the gag, and she nods at me as I press my cock through the silicone ring and onto her tongue. Holding the back of her head, I push forward slowly, forcing all of my cock into her mouth and down her throat. Holding her lips tight to my base for a moment, I pull back.

Drool rolls down her chin as she gasps for air. I bend down until our foreheads are touching and whisper, "That's the last one that will be gentle."

Standing, I grab the base of my cock and shove it back into her mouth as I fist the hair at the back of her head. Holding her head in place with the tight grip around her locks, I fuck her face. Forcing her to swallow me around her retches as her spit pours over her lips.

Releasing the grip in her hair, I pause my thrusts and grab hold of the chain running between the clamps on her tits.

"You're going to stay completely still while I fuck that gorgeous fucking face of yours," I give a firm tuck of the chain and she moans around the gag in her mouth, "or you're going to see just how tight those clamps can get."

Holding the chain in my left hand, I shove my cock down

her throat while bringing the chains of the flogger over the flesh of her ass.

Moaning, she recoils from the pain of the flogger, causing the chain of the clamps to pull tighter. She lets out a pained scream around my cock, but it only fuels my need to take her harder.

Bringing the flogger over her curvaceous ass, I strike her repeatedly until it's red and welts are forming as I continue to fuck her mascara-stained face.

Dropping the flogger and the chain, I twist my fingers into her hair as my hips twitch against her face, roaring as my cum pours down the back of her throat.

"Fuck," I growl pulling my cock from her, as I marvel at the beautiful, pained mess kneeling before me.

CHAPTER EIGHT

ELIZABETH

Watching Cameryn take Will's cock as she fell apart on my lap was fucking painful, but it's nothing in comparison to watching him splay her spent body on the bed as he climbs between her legs.

Positioning her so that he can continue to watch me as well, he shoves his perfect fucking cock back deep inside her.

My pussy throbs with need, and I squeeze my thighs, trying to calm the urge to lift my skirt and spread my legs. Squirming in my seat, I fight the desperate need to tend to my throbbing clit.

"Don't even think about touching that needy fucking cunt," Will grunts at me as his hips repeatedly drive into Cameryn's screaming body. "You fucking watch her take my cock, wishing I'd fuck your needy cunt like this."

Cameryn's hands claw at the sheets as she comes for him again.

I fucking hate her...

"Tell her how fucking good it feels," Will slows his hips and teases her with the long strokes of his cock, "how much you love my cock."

"He's so fucking big," she barely manages to get the words out through her labored breaths. "I can't get enough."

"That's right, baby," he groans against her neck, using the name because he knows it hurts me. "And you take every inch of it so fucking well."

Lifting his body from hers, he drives his cock into her so hard she yelps. My pussy clenches so fucking hard I think I might come. He continues to fuck her without abandon, bringing her to orgasm as my thighs continue to clench so hard that they are on fire.

"Please," I whimper with need as I watch Cameryn come again.

"So much as think about putting a hand on that needy pussy of yours before I give you permission, and you'll be going home still wanting and unsatisfied. Understood?"

"Yes," I groan, the urge to come practically painful.

I watch his long, thick cock slide in and out of her. Her tight pussy is visibly swollen from the abuse she is taking from the violent thrusts from his massive cock.

I wish he was destroying my cunt...

Or how eagerly I'd settle for my own thin finger at this point.

"Tell me, Cameryn," Will slows his thrusts, allowing her to catch her breath. "Do you enjoy the taste of another woman's pussy?"

When she doesn't answer, he leans close and teases his teeth along her neck. "Would you lick Liz's needy cunt as a thank you to me for ruining your cunt for all other men?"

"Yes," she answers, and both their eyes travel to me.

"Lift your skirt," Will stares at me as he continues to slide his length into her overused pussy, "and take off your panties."

I do as he says and step toward the bed, only to watch him shake his head.

"First, I'm going to make you watch me fill her tight little cunt with my cum," he increases the urgency of his hips. "Then, if I think you deserve it, I might give you the pleasure of sucking her from my cock as you ride her face."

My thighs clench tightly, but it does nothing to stop my arousal from running down them.

Will's hips quiver against her, a loud groan billowing from his chest, and I know he's finished inside of her.

Ruining almost any chance of him fucking me.

"Get on her face, baby girl," Will's tone is softer as he continues to leisurely work his length through his spilled cum.

Climbing onto the bed, my thighs straddle her face, hesitating to take more than Will has allowed.

"Show me how fucking grateful you are that she shared my cock with you," Will softly commands as he pulls himself from Cameryn's cunt. Her hands wrap around my thighs, and she drags me onto her mouth.

Her tongue dives into my pussy and over my clit. She licks, teases and sucks until my hips are grinding against her face.

It might be my neediness, but she eats a pussy nearly as well as she sucks a cock.

Will stands on the bed, his feet straddling Cameryn as he walks toward me with his cock in his hand.

"You want my cock, baby girl?" He rubs the wet tip over my lips, "Open wide and suck me clean."

Opening my mouth, he places his cock on my tongue. My tastebuds immediately overwhelmed with the tangy taste of Cameryn's pussy and the salty taste of Will's cum.

As I take him to the back of my throat, Cameryn sucks on my clit and the painful, much-needed, orgasm explodes through every nerve in my body. My body wound so tight with need, that every muscle trembles as it rocks through me.

Will pulls his cock from my mouth, and bends down to claim my mouth with his as I continue to ride out the last of my orgasm rocking over the length of Cameryn's tongue.

"Fuck, baby girl," he groans when he pulls back from our kiss. "No one fucking comes undone like you. You're so fucking perfect."

CHAPTER NINE

GRANT

Trying to focus on the woman beneath me, I'm repeatedly distracted by the screams coming from the couple in the grass at the far edge of the pool.

Chloe is stripped bare, face down, clawing at the grass beneath a nearly fully-clothed Samuel. His belt is cinched tight around her neck, silencing most of her screams, as he plows into her.

"That's it," he growls loudly. "Fucking fight me. You're so fucking tight when you scream."

Her hands clutch at the dirt beneath her, and she claws at the belt around her neck as he continues to have his way with her.

She fucking plays the part well.

Holding Madeline's jute braided hair, I thrust into her cunt from behind once more before pulling her face from the swimming pool.

Her cunt clenches around me like a fucking vise as she violently gasps for air.

"One more, dear," I press her head down until the tip of her nose is resting against the water as my fingers work her clit. "Come again and we'll be all done. Don't, and I'll hold you under until I've had my fill."

I give her a second to take a deep breath, then plunge her face into the water. My fingers diligently working her clit, I work my cock in and out of her cunt at an equally quick pace. The water bubbles around her submerged head and her pussy quivers around my length.

Pulling her from the water, I use the braid in my hand to sit her against my thighs as I relentlessly pound up into her.

"You did so fucking good for me," I groan against the back of her neck.

"No more," her words are deeply muffled from the ropes gagging her mouth. "I can't."

"You will." My fingers continue to pad over her clit as I fight back my own impending release. "I want you to be a quivering fucking mess when I finally fill you with my cum."

Her thighs shake and her cunt clenches around me. My balls tighten painfully hard, and I'm unable to fight it any longer. Feeling my cock become rigid inside of her, it spasms uncontrollably as I spill into her.

Pulling my softening cock from her, I undo the knot at

the nape of her neck. The moment the gag falls from her mouth, a blood-curdling scream exits her lungs.

Following her gaze, I find Chloe lying limp and lifeless in the grass at the far end of the pool. The belt previously cinched tight around her neck, now lax. Her blue lips agape and motionless.

"Fuck," Samuel's expletive is almost drowned out by Madeline's screams.

"Shut up," I fist the hair at the back of her head, but she continues to scream until I shove her face back beneath the water of the pool.

Her hands now free, she trashes hard, making waves in the previously still water.

"What the fuck is going on out here?" Liz yells as she strides onto the patio tiles surrounding the pool, just in time to watch me push Madeline's lifeless body into the water.

The others are only a few steps behind her, and Cameryn immediately screams at the sight of the dead woman in the grass and the other in the pool.

Stepping behind her, Will swiftly wraps his arms around her throat and breaks her neck with the precision of a man who has had ample practice. When he lets go, her body crumples at his feet.

He steps toward Paisley, who is eerily silent, fully prepared to eliminate her as an issue as well. He pauses when Edmund steps between the two of them.

"You don't need to worry about her," Edmund's voice is firm. "Do they, sweetheart?"

Her eyes wide, she vigorously shakes her head as Edmund continues, "I'll ensure she never says a fucking word about this."

"Maybe I should have been clearer earlier," Liz huffs, "I meant don't fucking kill any of them."

———

We've all always been deviant fucks, but that one night a year ago changed everything.

Using our collective skills and resources, we disposed of each of their bodies and removed every last digital trail of them.

No one cares when a ghost disappears.

Except maybe those that knew them.

Learning just how far we could go, the five of us have continued to test our limits in Adelaide Cove. Pushing the boundaries of our carnal urges, we've all delved further into the darkness inside of us.

As Charles Baudelaire once said, "The greatest trick the Devil ever pulled was convincing the world he didn't exist."

That's fucking bullshit.

The greatest trick he ever pulled was convincing the world there was only one of him.

Family

TIES

THE SAVAGELY DEPRAVED SERIES

FAMILY TIES

To everyone who wanted darker...

Buckle up,

We're just getting started.

CHAPTER ONE

ABIGAIL

"I'm serious, Garr," I huff at Garrison as I hastily shove the handful of panties into my suitcase.

"I'm serious, too," he smirks. "Make sure you pack that little black crotchless thing I like."

"Excuse you, sir." I lift the lacy black negligee from the drawer and hold it against me. "But this is not suitable attire for meeting one's future father-in-law."

"Trust me, he'd love it," Garrison mocks me as he swipes it from my hands and places it neatly in my suitcase. Wrapping his large arms around me and kissing along my neck, he whispers, "We both know I won't make it two days without fucking you, let alone a whole week. You're packing it."

"Fine," I exhale and practically feel his smug smile stretching across his face.

Pacing through the bedroom, I repeatedly open dresser drawers and flip through hangers in the closet, trying to figure out what it is that I'm forgetting.

"Really though." I fumble through a drawer. "What if he doesn't like me?"

"Abby." Garrison's voice is gruff as he sits on the edge of the bed.

"Garrison," I mock his tone before shrugging, "You don't get it. You've got more money than you could ever spend. You know how that looks when someone like me marries into that."

Like I'm a gold-digging whore...

Unlike him, I come from nothing. Less than nothing. Both my parents were significantly more concerned with getting their next fix than ensuring we had food on the table or a roof over our heads. Most of my childhood was spent sleeping on the backseat of the rusted Chevy Caprice or fighting off unwanted advances when we crashed with my parents' friends. I've eaten more meals from a dumpster behind a restaurant than I care to count.

As awful as it is to say, the best day of my life was when the two of them overdosed from a cheap fix laced with too much fentanyl. From that night on, I had a roof over my head and food to eat as a ward of the state.

"Hey." Garrison stretches out his hand for me to join him. "You are a talented and successful artist."

"No, I'm a starving artist mooching off her extremely rich fiancé." I take his hand and he pulls me between his thighs. His large hands wrap around my waist, and I stare down at him as I let out an exasperated sigh. "He's going to hate me."

"You're stressing about this way too much." Garrison's hands comfortingly rub over my hips.

"That's because you're not stressing about this nearly enough."

Without breaking eye contact with me, his fingers tip into the top of my jeans, swiftly undoing the button. Gripping the zipper, he takes his time lowering it.

"Garr" I playfully swat at his hand. "What are you doing?"

"Helping you relax, angel." His fingers slide beneath the silk of my panties.

"We don't have ti—" My words interrupted by my hitched breath as he slides two large fingers inside of me.

"We can be a little late." His fingers curl as he works against the tight confines of my skinny jeans to thrust them inside my pussy. Wrapping his other hand delicately around my throat, he pulls my face down to his to claim my mouth. The kiss is slow and deep, matching the fingers currently being used to pleasure me.

Whimpering as he pulls back from our kiss, my nails dig into his shoulders as he works me to the brink.

"Let go, angel." His words vibrate against my lips as he adds the pad of his thumb to my clit.

"Yes," I moan as I come, my thighs tremble around his hand so hard I struggle to stay standing.

Pulling his fingers from me, my body quivers when he slides them over my clit as he withdraws them from my pants. He pauses to wipe the wetness of my arousal on the bed sheets, lifts my zipper and rebuttons my pants. Standing from the bed, he grips my chin as he lifts my face up to his. "Feel better?"

"I mean, I don't feel worse," I smirk at him.

"I'll happily fuck you on the plane," he smiles. "And finger fuck you again at the main gate of the house when we get there if you start to get nervous again."

I jokingly shove him from me and turn to zip my suitcase on the bed.

"Wait." I turn to look at him. "There's a main gate? Does that mean there's more than one?"

Garrison's phone buzzes and he lifts it from the nightstand before saying, "The car is downstairs to take us to the airport."

"We aren't taking your car?"

"Dad insisted that we use his plane." He grabs the handles of both our suitcases.

"I'm sorry." I tilt my head, "Did you say *his* plane?"

And just like that, I'm anxious as hell again.

CHAPTER TWO

GRANT

Not sure how much Garrison and Abigail will be bringing with them for their week-long visit, I opt for the G-Class to pick them up from Parker Field. But based on the size of the wrapped package currently being unloaded from the plane, that was the right decision.

Exiting the car, I walk behind it and open the tailgate for the ground crew carrying their luggage.

Garrison steps from the door of the Cessna first. He flashes me a brief smile before turning to offer his hand to the woman he has brought home with him.

The breeze blows her lightly curled blonde hair across her face as she exits the plane. Lifting her hand to tuck her hair behind her ear, the sun glimmers across the massive diamond adorning her finger. That glimmer is nothing in comparison to the sparkle of her emerald-colored eyes. Pouty pink lips and a slightly upturned nose round out her face.

Reaching the bottom of the stairs, she steps beside Garrison, revealing the lean and curvaceous body that his body was hiding.

She's fucking magnificent.

"It's been too long, Garrison," I smile and extend my hand toward him as I approach the two of them. When he takes my hand, I pull him close for a hug. Patting my hand on his back, I whisper with a gruff tone with a hint of fury, "Way too fucking long."

Pulling back from Garrison, the smile on his face quickly fades when he realizes my displeasure at the length of time it has taken him to return to Adelaide Cove.

"And you must be Abigail." I turn my attention to the blonde with a broad smile.

A nervous smile spreads across her face. "Please feel free to call me Abby. It's a pleasure to finally meet you, Mr. Geyer."

"Abby, I'm going to have to insist that you call me Grant," I reply as I gently shake her small, soft hand. Holding onto it probably a tad longer than I should.

The ground crew closing the tailgate on the G-Class draws my attention, and I release her hand.

"As gorgeous of a day as it is, why don't we head to the house instead of getting to know each other out here on the tarmac?" I gesture toward the SUV.

Garrison's hand slides down the gentle curvature of

Abigail's back to lead her toward the car. Opening the front passenger door, he says, "I'll sit in the back."

"Don't be silly." She steps from his touch, moving toward the rear. "Sit up front with your dad. I'm probably going to be too busy drooling at the massive houses you told me about to be good conversation anyway."

Garrison closes her door and climbs into the front seat as I walk around the car. Climbing in, I ask, "How was your flight?"

"It was good," Garrison responds with a sincere nod.

"It was awfully generous of you," Abigail chimes in from the backseat.

"It was nothing." I glance in the rearview mirror to meet her eyes. "What is the point of owning planes if you aren't going to use them?"

"Planes?" Her eyebrow lifts inquisitively as she emphasizes the 's.' "As in *you* own more than one?"

Turning my attention back to the winding tree-lined roads before me, I respond, "The Cessna, which you flew in on, is good for shorter trips and landing at smaller airports like this one. The Challenger is much larger and designed for longer flights. Because of its size, it requires a runway able to handle a commercial airliner."

"Oh," her voice trickles off as we approach the sprawling mansions on the outskirts of town. Glancing at her in the rearview, her mouth is slightly agape as she stares out the window.

"Try not to get drool on the window," I jokingly address her.

"No promises," she quips. "These homes are downright incredible."

"They don't have homes like this where you're from?"

"Father," Garrison scowls as he nudges my arm.

"It's fine, Garr." Her voice is soft from the backseat. "He's going to find out eventually."

"As intrigued as I am to learn." I turn on the blinker to turn toward my estate. "Why don't we table this for a moment while we get everyone inside and situated? Then I can learn all about you over a drink by the pool."

Pulling up to the gate, I slow to allow the sensor in the car to register and slide the gate open.

"Welcome home." I pull through the gate as it opens. "It's going to be great having you here."

CHAPTER THREE

ABIGAIL

Stepping from the SUV, the home that stands before me is unlike anything I have ever seen. The massive mansion is a beautiful shade of cream-colored brick, accented with black windows and details scattered across the exterior. To the left of the house is a matching, large multi-car garage. Both are completely surrounded, with landscaping so perfect you'd think someone hand-cuts each blade of grass.

"Come." Grant stands at the bottom of the black steps leading up to the front door. "One of the staff will get your things."

"I'd really like to grab the gift if you don't mind." I begin to walk to the back of the SUV.

"Garrison will grab it for you." He tips his head at him. "Won't you, son?"

"Of course, Father," Garrison responds with an unusual tone.

"Come, Abby." Grant's voice is firm, yet welcoming. "Let's get you a drink, and Garrison will meet us out on the patio."

Meeting him at the bottom step, he places his hand on the small of my back and leads me up the steps toward the oversized double black doors. When I step inside, I am equally in awe of the décor as I was of the outside of the home.

"You have a beautiful home," I practically gasp. "It's perfect."

"It's your home too now, dear." He continues to guide me through the main room of the home and toward the French doors leading into the backyard. "And it's only almost perfect."

I'm about to question what he means when Grant asks, "What's your drink of choice, Abby?"

"A Tennessee Mule," I respond, watching his brow arch inquisitively.

"A whiskey girl," he smirks. "Not quite what I would've guessed."

"What? Did I strike you as a rosé girl?" I abruptly turn and am met with his chest. Fumbling against him, my hands on his pecs, I suddenly can't breathe. His large hand wraps around my wrist as I slowly step backward, trying to regain my composure. Gently pulling my hand from his light hold, I stammer, "I'm sorry."

What the fuck was that?

"Nothing to be sorry about, dear." His words slow and deep as he pushes open one of the French doors and gestures for me to go through.

As I walk the beautifully landscaped patio and take in the view of the Olympic-sized pool, Grant pulls out his phone. Standing at the edge of it, I stare across the never-ending view of the gardens.

I don't belong here...

A hand brushes down my spine, and I jump so hard I think I'm going to fall into the pool. As I teeter forward, a strong arm wraps around my waist and pulls me into a body.

"You're awfully jumpy, Angel," Garrison whispers in my ear as his fingers linger along the waistline of my jeans. "I offered to help you with that on the plane."

"Garr." I shove his hand from the top of my pants. "Of course, because I would love nothing more than for your dad to walk back out here and catch you knuckle deep inside me. Where did he go, anyway?"

"He went to get Victor."

"Victor?" I tip my head.

"The butler," he responds while ushering me to the table.

"The *butler*?"

"Abigail, since my son doesn't usually bring me wrapped gifts." Grant gestures to the large square covered in kraft paper as he steps back outside. "I'm assuming this is from you."

"Yes." I nod. "I mean, it's from both of us."

Grant slides a finger under the paper and carefully unwraps the canvas. He silently scans over the painting before him, taking in the swirls of greens intertwined with gold foil. His eyes move from the bottom right corner, over to me, and back to the canvas before he asks, "This is yours? You painted this?"

"Yes," I quietly respond. While proud of what I create, it's always difficult to put it out into the world.

"It's like staring into your eyes." He turns so that he can see both me and the painting at the same time. "Beautiful and absolutely fucking mesmerizing."

Heat creeps up my neck and over my cheeks, both from his words and the way he's looking at me right now.

A gaze that feels very inappropriate for your future daughter-in-law.

Considering how oblivious Garrison is to our current interaction, I shove the feelings away. Putting it down to nothing more than my nerves over this situation continuing to get the better of me.

"Your drinks, sir." An older gentleman, I assume is Victor, walks toward the table and sets down a small tray.

"Thank you," Grant responds as he hands him the painting. "Please take this to my bedroom and ensure it is hung for me."

"Of course, sir."

CHAPTER FOUR

GRANT

"This dinner was absolutely delicious." Abigail exclaims, after she practically licked her plate clean. "But tomorrow night, I would really like to make you both dinner."

"Could she be more perfect," I smile at her while nudging Garrison's elbow. "Smart, talented, beautiful, and she can cook."

"I mean, it won't be quite like this." She lifts her plate for Victor and silently mouths, "Thank you."

Even with her childhood, everything about her is just sweet and innocent.

We've been sitting on the patio for so long that the sun is beginning to set behind the tops of the trees surrounding the yard.

Taking a hefty sip of her wine, Abigail sets her glass on the table and proceeds to prop her chin up in her hands.

Her eyes continue to linger between Garrison and me for a few minutes before she speaks, "It's uncanny. The two of you, and how alike you look. Other than the gray hair... I mean... Shit! I think I might've had a glass too many."

"I thought women liked a silver fox," I smirk and watch as her already wine-flushed cheeks pinken a little more.

"I think it might be a good idea for me to head to bed before I stick my foot any further in my mouth." She stands, looks at the house, and turns back to the table. "And where would that be exactly?"

"It's been a long day; I'll come with you." Garrison also rises from his seat.

"No, let me." I join them in standing and place a hand on Garrison's shoulder, silently instructing him to take his seat, "We have a few things to talk about before you turn in for the evening."

I slip her arm into the crook of my elbow to help steady her imbalance from all the wine and walk her inside as Garrison takes his seat at the table.

That's a good boy..

"I really can't thank you enough. Ya know, for being so welcoming of me in your home," she rambles as I help her upstairs to the largest of the guest suites.

"It's your home now too." I open the door and lightly usher her inside. Lifting her chin, I place a soft chaste kiss on her lips before whispering, "I think you'll be quite happy here."

They're so fucking soft...

"Good night, Abigail." I watch her fingers linger over her lips as I speak, her eyes on mine as I step from the room and shut the door.

He did fucking good.

Maybe too fucking good...

I stand outside the door for a moment, merely thinking about how absolutely amazing she is. Realizing I need to return to a waiting Garrison, I walk from her room at the end of the hall.

"Father." Garrison is out of his seat when I exit the house. "We need to talk."

"Yes." I solemnly shake my head as I take the seat across from him, "We definitely do."

"Abigail is so much more than you described her as." I take a long sip of my old fashioned. "She might actually just be perfect."

"That's what we need to talk about." He folds his arms on the top of the table and leans toward me. "She is perfect."

"So, we agree? I don't think I could've picked better if I'd found her myself."

I watch Garrison slump back in his chair, his body language clearly telling me that he has more to say. I'm about to push the matter when my phone buzzes on the table.

EDMUND

> First, did Garrison and the girl arrive?
> Second, I think we have a problem with
> the kid.

"We'll talk more tomorrow, Garrison." I push up from the table as I read the text. "Business. I have to deal with this."

> Yes. They made it just fine. She's fucking incredible. You all are going to fucking love her.

Looking forward to meeting her. Soon I hope.

> What's the problem?

Rumor has it Detective Michales is investigating an assault that happened outside The Rusty Anchor.

I don't know it was him, but let's just say it sounds like his kind of party.

> What is his fascination with these fucking dive bars? Liz can procure literally anything he wants.

> Nothing is going to happen tonight. But I'll work on her record first thing in the morning.

> By the time I'm done, she'll just be the little whore that cried wolf.

I'll talk to him. Let him know you're getting tired of cleaning up his messes.

When do we all get to meet this incredible beauty.

Soon.

Real soon.

CHAPTER FIVE

ABIGAIL

Waking up, I feel for Garrison, but his side of the bed is cold. I roll over and see that his side of the bed was slept in. I grab my phone from the nightstand and take a glance at the time. *08:57.*

Garrison has probably been out of bed for at least an hour by now. I don't think I've ever seen him lounging in bed after eight.

Fuck...

I abruptly place my fingers on my lips when I remember the drunken moment last night.

Grant kissed me.

There was a lot of wine with dinner, and I was quite tipsy. I'm probably overthinking it. It was probably just an innocent kiss. It meant nothing.

It didn't feel like nothing though.

Merely thinking about it, I get the same tingle of excitement and need between my thighs that I did when his lips dusted over mine. A need I desperately want to tend to. Sliding my hand under the sheet, I run my fingers down the length of my stomach. I can't help but think how wrong this is as I push my fingers under the lace of my panties.

It's just like fantasizing about Jeffrey Dean Morgan, Eric Dane, or that silver fox on all those romance book covers...

My fingers slide over my pussy, and my panties are already fucking drenched.

He's just a much more mature version of your fiancé...

Sliding my fingers through my arousal, I slip one inside with a groan before sliding it over my clit. I tease over and around the hardened bundle of nerves with the pad of my finger until I am unable to contain my moans.

"Do you want some help with that, Angel?" Garrison stands in the now-open doorway.

"Fuck," I yelp as my eyes dart open. "You scared me half to death."

"Not what I asked." He closes the door and walks to the side of the bed. Gripping the sheets, he inches them down my body. "You still haven't answered my question."

Gently grabbing behind my knees, he pulls my ass to the edge of the bed.

"What were you thinking about?" His finger slides under

the lace and pulls my panties to the side as he kneels beside the bed. "Because you're never this wet for me."

Not a lie.

Garrison gets the job done in the bedroom, most of the time.

But he's never affected me quite like this.

"Henry Cavill?" I lie, coyly responding while shrugging my shoulders.

Okay fine, your father.

"Tell me." His tongue delicately licks up the length of my pussy. "Tell me what he was doing that you're this excited."

This is new...

"He was standing so close to me that we were practically touching." He repeatedly licks at my pussy. "His fingers slid under my chin, lightly gripping my jaw to tilt my face up to his."

Moving my hips, I try to guide Garrison's tongue to the place I want it. The place I need it.

"His lips pressed against mine. So soft that I almost couldn't feel them." His tongue grazes my clit and I struggle for a moment. "It wasn't enough, and I shoved my tongue into his mouth as he carried me to the bed."

Garrison's tongue licks fervently between my thighs, repeatedly narrowly missing the mark. Unintentionally edging the fuck out of me.

"Climbing over me onto the bed, he settles himself between my thighs." I lace my fingers into Garrison's hair. Fisting it tightly, I hold him in place as I work my clit against his tongue.

Hell...

My fiancé's face is buried between my thighs, and I'm moments from coming while he unknowingly listens to me tell him all about my fantasy of his father.

Going straight to fucking hell

"Fuck," I groan breathlessly as I grind my hips against his face.

With my eyes closed, I imagine the salt and pepper hair between my fingers. Grant devouring my pussy before sliding inside of me.

"Laying on top of me, he kissed and sucked across my chest." I struggle to get out each word as I creep toward my impending orgasm, "grinding every inch of his massive—"

My thighs tremble against the sides of Garrison's face as the orgasm wracks through my body. Holding him in place, my hips writhe against his tongue, practically forcing him to make me come again.

"Fuck, Angel," Garrison growls as I release my tight grip on his hair. His face is coated in my arousal when he sits back on his feet. "What's gotten into you?"

Your father...

"I'm fucking covered in you, hard as fucking hell." His hand rubs over the bulge in his pants. "And I don't have time to do anything about it."

"Are you coming?" Grant's voice carries through the door as he knocks gently.

"She was," Garrison whispers with a smirk as he stands between my thighs before shouting at the door. "I'll be down in a minute. I just need to change my shirt."

"Shit," I slap my hand over my mouth, "Do you think he heard me?"

CHAPTER SIX

GRANT

Standing at the guest bedroom door, my hand is on the knob. Every fiber of my being wanting to turn it and give Abigail more of what she obviously so desperately needs.

Releasing the doorknob, I slide my palm over the length of my hardened cock fighting for room in the confines of my pants. Not being able to put my cock inside her is only going to add to my frustrations this morning.

I've been up since dawn, dealing with the situation Edmund reached out about last night. Delving through digital files at the Adelaide Cove Police Department from the comforts of my home office, I found the woman from The Rusty Anchor. She's a twenty-six-year-old waitress living in a shit trailer in a questionable area of town, and from what I can gather, she has zero ties to Adelaide Cove. She lives with her five-year-old son, and I can't find a shred of information regarding his father. If it weren't for the kid, this could be a cheap as hell fix.

"Grab the bag." I tip my head to the floor as Garrison reaches the bottom of the steps. He grunts lifting the duffel bag as I walk out the front door and toward the awaiting SUV at the bottom of the steps.

"Where are we going?" Garrison questions as he climbs into the passenger seat.

"To take care of a problem." I slip the Tahoe into drive and begin to make my way across town. We ride in silence; his eyes fixated out the window at a part of town he has probably never seen before.

Pulling down a gravel road, I come to a stop before a rusted, single-wide trailer that probably should have been condemned ten years ago. Garrison turns toward me with an inquisitive look on his face when I put the SUV in park.

"Take the bag. Ring the bell and tell her the following: Nothing happened at The Anchor. You inherited some money, and you're going to start a new life for you and Tyler." I give him the instructions. "Don't give your name, and don't fuck this up."

He swallows hard and nods before retrieving the bag from the backseat. I watch as he tentatively walks up the rickety steps to the front door. A pretty, yet grossly underweight, brunette answers the door and she hesitantly takes the bag from Garrison. Placing the heavy duffle at her feet, she bends down to unzip it and pulls out one of the stacks of bound hundred-dollar bills. She nervously gives a few quick shakes of her head before pulling the bag inside and shutting the door.

Garrison climbs back into the car, and from the look on his face, it is apparent he has questions. He also knows his place and will not ask a single one of them.

One more stop before heading back home.

Pulling into the estate, the well-concealed front yard looks like he had a fucking frat party last night. I park at the front door, slide out of the car, and huff at Garrison, "Stay here."

Like the good son he is, he closes his door and re-fastens his seatbelt.

Ringing the bell, I hear Samuel shout, "Come in. It's open."

The noises coming from the other side of the door give me a good idea what's going on inside. When I push open the door, I'm met with the sight of a blonde woman's lips wrapped around his cock. Her eyes dart to me as he aggressively holds her head in place, forcing her to continue to suck his cock as I walk over.

"I can feel your fucking heart racing as I shove my cock down your throat," he snarls at the nervous woman on her knees before him. "Are you scared? Or maybe excited about having him fuck you too."

He drives himself into her throat and tears roll down her face as I approach the two of them. "Two powerful men, using and abusing you like the dirty little whore you are."

Reaching them, I wrap my hand around his throat. His cock slides from the mouth of the now gasping girl on the floor as I shove him against the wall. Pressing my weight against Samuel's body to hold him in place, I turn my attention to the girl, "Get the fuck out. Because when I'm done with him, I guarantee he will be taking it out on you if you're still in here."

I hear her scramble quickly from the floor as I throw a fist into Samuel's gut. Followed by three more to his face.

"I'm getting real fucking sick and tired of cleaning up after you," I seethe as I shove my forearm into his throat. "This was the last one. Understood? You can fucking rot in jail if you're this fucking careless again."

"You wouldn't." He swallows hard. "Because you'll all be there with me."

"Don't fucking threaten me, kid." I throw another punch to his gut and let him crumple down the wall to the floor. "And remember that dead men can't talk."

He doesn't get up or argue as I walk to the door because he knows better than most people that I have zero qualms about putting another dead body in the ground. Slamming the front door as I exit, I stalk toward the Tahoe and slide back into the driver's seat.

I can feel the heat in my face as I boil with anger. My current level of frustration needs desperately to be dealt with.

"Father?" Garrison sheepishly questions from the seat beside me, "We really need to talk about Abby."

"Does now really seem like a good fucking time for that?" I snarl as I pull into traffic and head home.

"No, Father." He drops his head and sulks in silence the remainder of the way home.

CHAPTER SEVEN

ABIGAIL

The front door slamming startles me from the waffles, strawberries, and cream the chef was kind enough to whip together for me this morning. Looking up, I watch as Garrison storms past the dining room before I hear him stomp up the steps like an upset child.

"What's up with him?" I question Grant when he walks into the dining room.

"He'll be fine." His voice is deep and has a tinge of his accent as he pulls out the chair beside me. "Mind if I join you?"

"Of course not," I mumble around the forkful of food I just shoved in my face.

"I know we left you alone all morning, but do you think you can occupy yourself the rest of the day? Garrison and I have some business that we need to discuss."

"I mean, I was going to take advantage of this gorgeous weather. A little time sunbathing by the pool, and maybe enjoying a leisurely swim," I respond, and I swear I catch a glimmer of excitement in his eyes.

"Good." A smirk ticks up the corner of his mouth, and he watches as I shovel another mouthful of my late breakfast into my mouth.

"You've got a little…" His hand reaches toward me, and my breath sputters as he lightly grips my jaw. Slowly swiping his thumb along the corner of my mouth, he pulls back and displays the small bit of cream he collected.

He stares back at me, his deep blue eyes bore through me as he slips his thumb between his lips and sucks it clean.

Is he flirting with me?

It definitely feels like he's flirting with me.

Withdrawing his thumb from his mouth, Grant stands from his seat and begins walking from the table.

I should say something…

"Mr. Gey…I mean, Grant," I call after him, but when he turns around I suddenly feel like an idiot.

What if it's nothing, and then I'm the one that makes this weird?

"Is the pool warm?" I struggle to come up with something to ask him.

"It's perfect. I enjoy using the pool year-round, and ensure it's always at an enjoyable temperature."

"Maybe if the two of you finish early, you can join me for a swim then." The words vomit from my mouth, and I watch as an odd smile spreads across Grant's face.

"Not today, but I would more than enjoy a swim with you."

Sitting alone again, I finish up my breakfast. After rinsing my plate and putting it in the dishwasher, I head upstairs to throw on my bathing suit.

Garrison is still having a moment when I walk into our room. I reach my hand out to rub his shoulder, but he pulls away from me when I ask, "Is everything all right?"

"Not now," he snarls as he storms into the adjoining bathroom.

Fine, but you aren't going to ruin my day.

Digging through my suitcase, I pull out my swimsuit and toss it on the bed before stripping off my clothes. I finish tying the top half of the bikini around my neck when Garrison walks from the bathroom. The moment of serenity on his face has immediately gone the second his eyes rake over my body.

"You're not fucking wearing that down to the pool." His voice is filled with a tone of anger I have never heard from him before.

"One, this was more than an acceptable bathing suit when we went to Key West a couple weeks ago. Two, it's the only one I packed." I pause to tie my sarong around my waist. "And three, you can fuck off if for a moment you think you're going to tell me what I can and cannot wear."

Before he has a moment to say a word, I grab my headphones and phone, ensuring that I am the one to be storming out of the room.

What the fuck has gotten into him?

Stopping to grab a bottle of water from the fridge, I head out to the pool. This backyard is like an oasis. So private and serene. If I was here alone, I'd be tempted to sunbathe nude to forgo any tan lines. As the thought runs through my mind, I look up to find Grant standing in what I assume is his office window.

Is he watching me?

Garrison joins him in the large window, and I can practically feel the tension between the two of them from here.

I reach for the knot on my sarong, and I can feel Garrison's eyes on me as my fingers work it. I meet his gaze through the window and stare into his eyes as I untie it. Defiantly dropping the sarong to the patio, I flip him the bird before pulling on my headphones and getting comfortable on one of the lounge chairs.

Paramore blares through my headphones as I shut my eyes. Trying desperately not to think about Garrison or Grant, and how much both are riling me up—in two very different ways.

CHAPTER EIGHT

GRANT

"She's fucking magnificent." My eyes never leave the curves of Abigail's body as Garrison enters the room. Her long hair is pulled into a messy bun atop her head. Her long, curvaceous body is adorned with a black string bikini and a sheer white wrap tied around her waist. Through the wrap, I can faintly see the crease where her ass meets her thighs, it's barely covered by the black bottom of her suit. As she turns, the faint outline of her tight nipples can be seen poking against the thin fabric.

Maybe I should've taken her up on that swim.

Garrison joins me in the window, and he audibly sighs when he realizes how intently I'm watching her.

"She's what I need to talk to you about." His voice is timid.

Realizing we're both watching her, Abby's eyes fixate on Garrison as she slowly undoes the wrap around her waist. Letting it fall to the ground, she flips him off before turning her attention away from us both.

"She's everything you said she was and more." I leave the window and make my way to the chair at my desk. "She's stunning. Smart. Funny. And apparently doesn't feel like she needs to put up with your shit. What did you do to piss her off anyway?"

"I told her not to wear the bikini." His tone is miffed as he takes a seat across from me. "I'd rather you didn't look at her the way you are."

"Is that so?" I snidely question.

"I want to discuss our arrangement." His gaze fixes on the floor as he continues, "I love her."

"You fucking love her?" My question is drenched in sarcasm, "Like you loved that woman you knocked up a month ago? While you were dating Abigail?"

"That was a mistake," he grumbles, "Are you going to hold that over my head?"

"I'm not holding anything over your head but our arrangement. But I can tell you with certainty that you don't fucking love her," I snarl.

He jumps from his chair, preparing to argue, and I yell, "Sit the fuck down. You love the fucking idea of her, but I can guarantee you love the fat fucking check I put in your account every month more."

Standing, I round the desk, walk to the door, and pull it open before lowering my voice. "If you love her more than my money, I'll see you at breakfast. If not, I expect you gone by the morning."

He crosses the room and stops when he reaches me. I wait for him to say something, but he cowers as usual and sulks out the door.

He might be a good boy, but he sure as fuck doesn't stick up for himself like a man.

Closing the door, I take a seat at my desk and spin the chair until I am facing the window overlooking the pool. Abigail has tired of sunbathing and is currently swimming leisurely laps in the pool.

Her long, lean legs flutter as she slides through the water. The tiny suit barely covering her now, I can't get enough of her round ass. It would look fucking gorgeous with my ropes wrapped around it.

Fuck...

My cock hardens at the thought and immediately tents my pants. Undoing my belt and zipper, I free it from its confines and stroke it slowly as I watch her below me in the pool.

Spitting in my hand, I tighten my grip as she pushes herself up on the edge of the pool and exits it. Beads of water roll down her body. Over the tight nipples protruding against the top of her suit, and down the bare flesh of her pert ass.

What I would give to shove her back in that pool and have my way with her.

Pulling the strings of her suit top until it falls from her body and into my hands. Wrapping the wet polyester around her wrists, binding them behind her back. The position puts her round, perky tits on full display. Defenseless as I pull the strings of her bottoms and let them fall between her feet.

Stroking faster as I continue to watch her through my fantasy.

Carrying her into the pool, her legs wrap around my waist as I claim every inch of her mouth with my tongue. Preparing it to be claimed by my cock. Taking us both to the deep end, I hold the ledge with one hand as I unwrap her legs from me.

"Deep breath, kitten." I grip her shoulder and firmly shove her under the water, not stopping until her mouth is wrapped tightly around my cock. She swallows every inch of me, trying desperately to make me come before...

"Fuck," I groan as warm cum splatters over my hand, way earlier than I had intended.

Kitten?

Interesting.

Suits her.

As I tuck my cock back into my pants, I watch Abigail walk back into the house. Holding the sarong in her hand, her ass jiggles with each pad of her feet. It's nearly enough to make me hard again.

Soon enough, kitten.

Garrison is nothing if not predictable.

CHAPTER NINE

ABIGAIL

I haven't seen Garrison since I told him to fuck off over the swimsuit. Dinner has come and gone. At least eating dinner with Grant was enjoyable. The sun set hours ago, and each of my texts has gone unanswered.

I'm desperately trying to stay awake for his return, but the rain pounding against the windows is making it pretty futile. The only reason I haven't fully drifted off yet is the occasional clap of thunder that draws my eyes open.

Unable to sleep, I head to the kitchen. I probably should've thrown something over the silk slip I was wearing in bed, but at this late hour, I figure no one will be around to see me.

Stepping into the kitchen, I reach for the light switch when a voice from the darkness of the room startles me.

"Leave it off, Angel," Garrison's voice a deep whisper. "I'm sorry."

Before I can respond, his hands are on my hips, and he hoists me onto the counter of the large island. Pushing the silk up my thighs, he bends between them. "Let me show you how sorry I am."

He shoves his face between my thighs; his tongue presses inside of me before sweeping up my slit. He licks and sucks at me until my fingers are gripping the granite beneath me. My hips rock against his face, and I whimper as he brings me to the brink.

Sucking at my clit, he gingerly squeezes two fingers inside of me. The moment he begins to curl them against my walls, I scream out his name as I come undone.

Hoping desperately that the raging storm outside has muffled my screams, I pull his face from me and up to my lips. I can taste me on his tongue as he plunges it into my mouth. My fingers work his belt, needing to have him inside of me.

Freeing him from his pants, I wrap my legs around his waist and pull him into me.

"Fuck." He nuzzles his face into my neck as he slides himself in and out of me. "I'm so fucking sorry."

A loud boom of thunder startles me, and when the lightning flashes through the room I swear I see Grant watching us from the doorway.

"Garr..."

Another boom.

Another flash, but Grant is no longer in the doorway.

"Shhh." The lips on my neck kiss down to my collarbone and back up to my ear before whispering, "You're mine now."

Suddenly, the man between my thighs isn't Garrison. My legs are wrapped tightly around Grant's waist as he drives every inch of him inside me so hard, I can't stifle my cries.

"Grant," I call out his name, my tone a mixture of pleasure and bewilderment.

"Mine, Abigail," he grunts, slamming into me again, and I claw at his back as I come undone.

Screaming in pleasure as I come, Grant only picks up his speed and intensity. My thighs quiver against his waist as he forces me to come again.

BOOM!

I sit up straight in bed, my thighs twitch, and my breathing is so heavy that I can barely catch my breath.

Fuck. That felt so real.

A flash of lightning momentarily illuminates the room, and I see that I'm alone.

I think...

Still trying to catch my breath, I turn toward the nightstand and feel for the lamp. My fingers flick the switch, and I look around the room to find that I am indeed alone.

Garrison never came to bed last night. His side of the bed is still perfectly made. A black envelope with my name written on it sits on his pillow. Opening it, I pull out a heavy, white card with two words written on it.

I'M SORRY.

You couldn't even wake me to say you're sorry?

Climbing from bed, I head into the bathroom before finding him to hash this all out and put it behind us. As I groggily walk past the sink, I notice that his things are gone.

There's no trace of him in the bedroom either. No shoes. His suitcase is no longer sitting in the corner. Pulling open the closet door, none of his things are in there either.

Did he fucking up and leave in the middle of the night?

Who the fuck brings their fiancé to meet their parents and then abandons them?

Without saying a single fucking word?

Over a tiny fucking argument about a bathing suit?

What the fuck, Garr?

Needing to scream or cry, maybe both, at him, I storm back to my nightstand for my phone. But it isn't there. Bending down, I check underneath it and the bed to no avail. Wondering if maybe I fell asleep with it in the bed, I begin feeling the sheets and stripping the mattress. Still no phone.

Did I bring it upstairs after dinner?

Not needing last night's dream to come true, I stop myself from storming downstairs in my silk nighty. I rush to the bathroom to grab a robe. After throwing it on, I run my fingers through my hair before going to look for my phone.

Grabbing the knob of the door, I attempt to twist it, but it only jiggles in my hand.

CHAPTER TEN

GRANT

Even through the tumultuous storm last night, I heard Garrison creeping around the house and leaving around two in the morning.

Nothing, if not predictable.

Making my way down the hall toward Abigail's room, I can hear her jiggling the handle trying to open the door. Stretching out my hand to the knob, it opens, and she startles at finding me on the other side of the threshold.

"Have you seen Garrison?" she sputters, "Or maybe my phone?"

She steps backward as I let myself into the room, her eyes widen when I push the door shut behind me.

"Grant," her timid voice cracks as she says my name.

I continue to slowly stalk toward her as though she is my prey, and she continues to retreat. Her chest rising and falling with each slow, hesitant step. When her back hits the wall, I can't miss the twinkle of excitement and fear in the emerald eyes that are locked on me.

Taking a final step, my chest is inches from hers as I tower over her. I slide my fingers behind the belt holding her robe shut, and she swallows hard when I begin to undo the knot.

"Grant," she whispers. "We can't.... Garrison..."

"Garrison and I have an arrangement." I untie the first of the knots. "And I've already waited far too long to take what's mine."

"Yours? An arrangement?" she stammers as she tries unsuccessfully to step from the wall.

"He finds me beautiful, young women. Women without families. Little to no friends." I undo the second knot and let the belt fall to her sides. "Women that won't be missed."

Her chest heaves, and I can almost read the range of emotions across her face and in her eyes as I unbuckle and unzip my pants. Sliding my hands between the slit in her robe, she is motionless with shock as I part it. A small growl grumbles from my chest at the sight of the short silk slip it was hiding and her tight nipples poking against the thin fabric.

"I paid him to find me a new pet." I grip her ass, before roughly pulling her left thigh over my hip. I can smell the arousal dripping from her bare cunt as I press my free hand between us to pull my hard cock from my pants.

Pressing every inch of me inside her, I growl, "You're mine now, kitten."

With one hand on her hip and the other holding her knee over my hip, I drive repeatedly into her slick perfection. Tears well in her eyes, but they don't fall down her cheeks.

"My pet. To play with as I please," I grunt, as I continue to take her hard and fast. She tries to stifle it, but she clenches around my cock as a whimper blows from her lips.

"Don't fight it." I squeeze her hip relentlessly hard as I thrust into her, "We both know you've been thinking about my massive cock inside of you since you got here. And you fucking love how I stretch out that tight little cunt of yours."

She suddenly fights against my grip, her hands flail as she futilely tries to shove me from her. Her hand strikes my face, nails raking down my cheek, and I hiss, "My kitten has claws."

Grabbing her hands, I take both her wrists in one hand and slam them into the wall above her head. She winces at the impact and momentarily stops fighting me. Snaking my free hand between her back and the wall, I squeeze her tightly and spin us both toward the bed.

I drop us both to the mattress without my cock leaving her tight cunt. Pinning her wrists above her head, I wrap my other hand around her throat. I squeeze my fingers enough to limit her ability to breathe, relishing in the feel of her rapid pulse beneath them.

"My pet will learn to play nice." My teeth graze her skin as I pull the silk from her nipple before sucking it into my mouth. Tightening my grip around her throat, I suck hard at the fleshy bundle of nerves. Her stifled moans vibrate against my fingers as my teeth slide over her already bruising flesh. "My kitten will behave, or she will be punished."

Loosening my fingers around her throat, I bury my cock inside of her. Thrusting hard and fast, my words deep and gravelly as I command, "You're going to come for me because you can't deny how fucking good it feels to finally have me inside you."

Continuing to demandingly slide my length in and out of her slick channel, she blissfully squeezes around my cock. A tear rolls down her cheek, and breathy moans rattle from her as she comes undone with me inside her.

Fucking perfection...

"That's a good little pet." I lick the tear from her face. "You're going to come for me again. And I expect to hear how fucking grateful you are that I've allowed you the pleasure of coming."

Lifting my body, I vigorously rub the pad of my thumb over her clit while relentlessly driving my cock into her. She clenches around me, and her body trembles beneath me as I force her to come again.

She feels so fucking good coming around my cock.

"Thank you, Sir." I groan the words for her to repeat. In turn, she purses her lips and shakes her head. Pulling my hand from her clit, I lightly slap her cheek and repeat the phrase, "Thank you, Sir."

She only squeezes her lips tighter and continues to shake her head.

Have it your way...

CHAPTER ELEVEN

ABIGAIL

Grant slaps my cheek, and groans the words again, "Thank you, Sir."

He has already taken my consent from me.

While I cannot fight the pleasure or orgasms he is bringing me, I refuse to give him this.

"Maybe I wasn't clear that bad pets will be punished." He stills his hips, keeping himself buried to the hilt. Parting the lips of my pussy, he drips a generous amount of saliva on my clit and smirks as he smears his thumb through it.

He teases my sensitive clit. Alternating between vigorous circles and feathered touches, repeatedly bringing me to the edge and painfully pulling me back.

"That's eight," he snarls as the corner of his mouth ticks up. "Two more, and then I'm going to fill you with my cum and mark this perfect little cunt as mine."

Two...I can't.

My thighs shake, and my clit feels like it's on fire. The need to come is absolutely painful.

I didn't realize it could get worse.

He takes his time, teasingly bringing me to the edge of my ninth denial. Panting with need, it is not lost on me that he is thoroughly enjoying every minute of this. Although completely unmoving, he is still rigidly hard inside of me.

It's too much.

"Please, Sir," I desperately plead as his thumb begins to rub over my clit again.

"That's good, kitten." He rubs hard and fast, and my hips writhe against his touch.

Finally.

Just as I am about to come, he pulls himself from inside me and denies me his touch again.

"You're learning." He begins to vigorously fist his length as he sits between my thighs, quickly working himself toward release. "But neither of us is going to get what we want."

Continuing to violently work his fist, he presses his tip inside of me. I try to move my hips to take in more of him, but he pulls back in return, refusing to slide into me.

"I'm still going to mark this cunt with my cum," he grunts the words between the quick strokes of his fist. "I just won't have the pleasure of being buried deep inside of you."

His hips sputter against his hand, and careful not to press further inside of me, he fills me with his cum with a loud groan. Pulling himself from me, he holds my thighs apart as he stares down at the mess that he made inside of me.

"You look fucking gorgeous dripping my cream, kitten." He stands from the bed and tucks his spent dick back into his pants. Pulling me to my feet, he gives a solitary command, "Come."

I fucking wish...

Grant's cum trickles down my thighs as he forcefully leads me down the hall. Abruptly stopping at an open door, I gasp when I see inside. It is filled with ropes, sex toys of all shapes and sizes, and various other types of restraints.

Pushing me inside, he pulls the already falling robe from me and drops it to the floor. Grabbing a neatly bound red rope in one hand, his other holds my arms behind my back. Holding my wrists, he begins weaving the rope between my arms, binding them together as he devilishly whispers, "Just need to ensure you aren't tempted to take care of that aching cunt of yours."

My arms bound behind my back, I watch as he meanders down the wall, stopping at a black leather collar. Returning to me, he slides my hair out of the way and fastens it around my neck. He looms over me as he hooks a gold chain to the loop at the front of the collar.

I really am his fucking pet...

"Are you going to make me crawl now too?" My tone is sassy as I try to retain any shred of power I still have.

"Mmmm, kitten," he slides his thumb over my lower lip, "By the time you're done learning your lesson, you will be crawling to me as you beg for my cock."

"Doubtful," I spit. I have zero desire for him to violate me again.

"We'll see." He grabs the leather loop at the end of the chain, and drags it hard, making me follow him from the room. Following closely behind him, he leads me into his office and takes a seat at his desk. He tips his head toward the floor, "On your knees. Sit still and be quiet."

I tentatively drop to my knees beside his office chair, and he loosens the slack of the chain around my neck. Picking up the phone, his free hand gingerly strokes my hair. I am about to scream for help to the person on the other end of the call when I hear them. "How's the girl? Abigail? I believe was her name?"

It's more than just Grant and Garrison?

"Fucking perfection," he answers them with sincerity as he turns his gaze toward me. "My little kitten is feisty, but she's fucking perfection."

He turns his phone toward me and takes a picture, which I assume he sends to the man on the other end of the call.

"If you need help taming her," his voice trails off.

He wouldn't...

"She's too perfect to let you ruin just yet." Grant strokes my face before continuing to pet my hair. "But I can only imagine how gorgeous she would be stuffed full of cock."

He would...

What wouldn't he do?

I need to get the fuck out of here.

CHAPTER TWELVE

GRANT

Finishing the call with Edmund, I make a quick call to Liz to ensure she is up to speed with things.

"You caught me at a bad time." Liz's breathing is labored, and I can clearly hear the sounds of Will and another woman in the background. "But if he continues to be a problem, we'll take care of him."

After I let her know that Samuel's problem has officially left town, she abruptly hangs up the phone.

Turning in my chair, I grip Abigail's face and tilt it up to mine. "Spread your thighs for me."

She hesitates, and I ask, "Are you going to learn how to obey me?"

Instead of answering, she poses her own question, "Are you going to kill me?"

"That's up to you, kitten." I tenderly slide my knuckles

down her jaw and watch as her knees slide wider on the hardwood floor. "But I'd rather not."

I don't get off killing women.

When it happens, it's solely the means to an end.

But I have no use for a disobedient pet that I can't fuck as I please.

Gripping the collar to hold her in place, I slip my fingers over her still hardened clit. Her eyes roll as a heavy sigh blows over her lips. I work her to the cusp of an orgasm before pulling my fingers from her and returning to my work.

I repeatedly edge Abigail between my work for hours. She is practically sitting in a puddle of her own arousal as I slide my fingers from her denied cunt once again.

"Please," her voice pained as she begs. "I'm sorry, Sir."

"Up" I grip Abigail's upper arms to help lift her from the ground. Pushing the papers immediately in front of me to the side of the desk, I grip her waist and hoist her onto the desk. Grabbing the scissors from the drawer, I cut the straps to her nightgown. I grip the silk between her breasts and slide the shears through the fabric until she is left wearing nothing but my collar around her neck.

"Does my kitten need to come?"

"Yes, Sir." Her eyes are full of need.

Placing my hands on her thighs, I slowly spread her thighs apart. Delighted at the sight of her cunt still dripping the remnants of my cum.

"Do you want to come on my tongue or cock?"

"Whatever you prefer, Sir."

Such a good kitten...

Lifting her legs, I place them over my shoulders. She moans as I hold her ass and pull my chair toward the desk to position myself against her cunt as I groan, "I have no qualms about licking my cum from your cunt if it means I get to taste you finally."

Spreading her wide, I lick the length of my tongue over her clit. Tasting her sweet arousal mixed with my salty release with each swipe of my tongue.

"Fuck, kitten," I groan against her. "You taste so fucking good."

My fingers dig into the flesh of her ass hard enough to leave bruises as I pull her tighter to my face; her hips rock against my tongue as more moans and whimpers spew from her mouth.

"Yes," she groans, and her feet dig into my back. Her whole body trembles as every denied orgasm crashes through her at once.

"Thank you, Sir." She pushes out the words through her labored breaths before I've fully removed my tongue from her clit.

I'm already hard as hell from making her come, but her sudden obedience deserves to be rewarded.

"For being such a good little pet, you're going to have the pleasure of coming on my tongue and my cock," I speak the words as I hastily shed my shirt and remove my pants.

Sliding her from the desk, I spin her around on her unsteady legs and gently lay her face down on my desk. As soon as her chest touches the desk, I kick her feet wider and step between them before sliding my cock into her dripping cunt.

Taking my time, I work myself in and out of her and undo the knots binding her arms together. Leaving her bound much longer will likely result in damage to her nerves. She groans as I release the final knot, allowing her arms to fall to her sides on the desk. Her skin is dimpled with the marks of the rope.

Rubbing my hands over her tender flesh and sore muscles, I bend over until I am pressed against her back. My mouth travels down her cheek, stopping to kiss her neck, and I whisper in her ear, "I intend to come like I wanted to this morning. Buried deep in your cunt, with you screaming out my name as I stare into those gorgeous fucking eyes of yours.

Pulling from her, I turn her onto her back before driving my cock back into her. Her emerald eyes bore into me as I continue to fuck her cunt. She slides further over the desk away from me with each demanding thrust, until I'm forced to grab her hips and drag her back to me.

Her already tight cunt quivers around my cock, and I fight against my release until I make her come again. Her back arches from the desk and squeezes around me so tightly that I couldn't hold back any longer if I tried.

"Mine," I growl, burying myself inside her as I come.

CHAPTER THIRTEEN

ABIGAIL

Tucking himself back into his pants, Grant retakes his seat in his chair before pulling my naked body onto his lap. His arm wraps around my waist, his thumb rubbing over my hip as his other hand tucks my hair behind my ear and places my head on his shoulder.

"See how well I'll reward you." He continues to stroke my hair. "When you're an obedient little pet."

You're just playing along, Abby.

"Yes, Sir," I force out the words.

Feeding into his twisted delusions for your own safety.

"Thank you." I swallow hard, fighting back the urge to vomit as I thank him for the pleasure of being violated. But the bile rising in my throat is also due in part to the small sliver of me that found enjoyment in the moment. Not the unwanted pleasure from orgasms he forced upon me, but actual gratification in the way he seeks to own me.

Fuck, Abby...

"Let's get you cleaned up, kitten." Grant slips his arms under my legs and stands. Carrying me down the hall, he doesn't take me back to my room. Instead, he takes me to his.

The moment he steps through the door of the massive suite, my eyes are immediately drawn to the corner. In it sits a large, ornate, iron bird cage—only it is massive. Way too big for any bird I have ever seen.

But the perfect size for a person...

"Is that where you're going to keep me?" I feel the tears pooling in the corners of my eyes.

"For now." He looks into my eyes as he responds, and the coldness in them chills me to the bone.

Leading me into the bathroom, he turns the knob to draw a bath and pours in some bubbles. As the large tub slowly fills, he strips from his clothes. Once he is undressed, he turns me to unfasten the collar around my neck. Placing it gently on the counter, he takes my hand as he steps into the tub.

"Get in." He lightly tugs at my hand, and I step into the hot bath water with him. Gently pulling me down with him, he situates me between his thighs so that my back is pressed against his chest.

Grabbing a large natural sponge, he dips it into the water and drags it tenderly over my chest. His touch is completely devoid of being sexual. Instead, it's sensual and intimate. No one has ever touched me like this.

Get it together, Abby.

"How long?" I barely muster the question.

"How long for what, kitten?" he whispers against my ear as he slides the soft sponge over my stomach.

"The cage." My lower lip trembles as I speak. "How long will you keep me in the cage?"

"I'm a patient man, Abigail. However long it takes."

"It takes?" I repeat his final words to him.

"For you to concede that you belong to me." He rubs the sponge up my neck, forcing my head to tip back onto his shoulder, "Some women take days. Others take months."

Others...

Even submerged in the steaming hot water of the bath, goosebumps prickle over my skin.

"We both know you're faking it now," his voice devilish as he whispers in my ear. "But eventually you'll break. They all do."

He continues with the sponge, as though he didn't just drop an absolute bomb on me, until he has cleaned every inch of my skin. He scoots me forward, his fingers lightly wrap under my chin, and he tips my head back. The warm water of the bath pours over my scalp and down my back. It is immediately replaced by his fingers, massaging shampoo into my hair. Once he is content that it's clean, he rinses it before repeating the process with conditioner.

Standing behind me, he steps from the water and wraps a towel around his waist. As if this is completely normal, he grabs another and takes my hand, helping me out before drying me with the same thoroughness that he cleaned me. Once I'm dry, he wraps the towel around me, combs, and dries my hair.

Sliding my hair over my left shoulder, he lifts the collar from the counter and pulls it back up to my throat. After fastening it, he lifts a small lock from the counter, and I hear it click behind my neck.

"Mine." He places a soft kiss on the back of my neck, just above the collar, before leading me into the bedroom.

Opening a drawer to the dresser, he pulls out a lacy black tank top, emerald-green satin shorts, and a matching robe. "I thought these might really bring out your beautiful eyes."

He places them on the bed, leaving me to get dressed as he pulls out new clothes of his own. I waste no time pulling them on, a futile attempt at covering myself and taking back a shred of my power.

Crossing the distance between us, he grips my chin and tilts my head up until I meet his gaze before placing a soft kiss on my lips. It both turns my stomach and arouses me.

There shouldn't be. But there is something about his touch.

"You look fucking beautiful, kitten." His lips vibrate against mine as he hovers from his kiss, "Are you hungry?"

"No." I shake my head, too nauseated at myself to even think about eating right now.

"I have things I need to tend to." He walks me to the large cage in the corner. "I'll be back for dinner."

He places a soft kiss on my cheek and shuts the door to the cage with the same nonchalance as kissing your wife goodbye before heading to work. He clicks the lock in place and walks from the room.

Leaving me caged—both in my new prison and with my thoughts.

CHAPTER FOURTEEN

ABIGIAL

There are no clocks on the walls, and the alarm clock on the nightstand is at an angle I cannot quite read. I have no idea how long I have been confined in here. Regardless of how long it has been, it feels like hours.

I've played with the lock, tried to squeeze myself through the bars, tried finding a way out of here. Giving up, I lay on the small couch to wait for Grant to come and release me.

The knob jiggling on the door startles me, and I am surprised when a woman walks in. She appears to be in her fifties, dressed in a uniform similar to a hotel housekeeper and is carrying a small bucket filled with cleaning supplies. Her eyes meet mine, and as though I am invisible, she proceeds with the tasks she came in here for.

"Ma'am," I whisper loudly. "Please."

Dusting the shelves and properly making the bed, she

passes mere feet from me numerous times but never looks at me.

"Please," I beg quietly. "Help me."

She continues to ignore me and my pleas for help as she meticulously cleans the room. When she finishes, she grabs her bucket to leave. Passing by the cage, she mumbles, "Just do as he says, honey. It'll be for the best."

"Ma'am," I shout as she walks from the door. "Please! Just help me!"

My hands slide down the metal bars of my prison as I crumple to the floor. Squeezing the cold metal between my fingers, my head rests against my hands as tears uncontrollably roll down my face and silent sobs rattle my chest.

There isn't a soul around that will save me.

I'm going to die here.

Tears continue to flow for so long that the sun is beginning to set by the time they finally dry up. Climbing from my crumpled position on the floor, my whole body is sore as I stretch my limbs.

Heavy footsteps in the hallway draw my attention. Loudening with each step, they rapidly approach the door to the bedroom. The door swings open and Grant walks through. His eyes meet mine, and I can see his disapproval of what I am assuming are my puffy, blood-shot eyes.

"Kitten." His voice is soothing and sympathetic as he unlocks the cage. Stepping inside, he pulls me up into his embrace. Stroking my hair and peppering kisses across my forehead, he whispers, "I don't like you crying."

"Please." The trembling word leaves my mouth before I can stop it.

I want to beg him to let me go, but the housekeeper's words keep playing through my head on repeat...

"Just do as he says, honey. It'll be for the best."

He eyes me suspiciously, waiting for me to say more.

"Please don't leave me in there." I burrow my face against his chest. "I was so worried you weren't coming back."

"Be good for me. Let me play." His hand roams over my ass and under the loose satin shorts. "And I'll let you stay out for a while."

"Thank you, Sir." I lift my head as I respond. As much as it pains me to admit, I am truly grateful for even an extra minute that he won't have me locked in there.

"You must be starving." He releases his embrace on me and begins to lead me to the door. "Dinner is waiting in the dining room."

As he walks me downstairs, I expect to be greeted with pet bowls in the corner. Eating on the floor as I watch him enjoy a gourmet meal at the table. Thankfully, I'm wrong, and I'm pleased to see two settings at the table when we enter.

Grant takes the seat at the head of the table and pulls me onto his lap.

Maybe I was wrong...

Gripping my leg, he pulls it over his knee until I am straddling his thigh before pulling the second plate of food in front of us.

"Eat up, kitten." He hands me a fork with a slightly threatening glare. "You're going to need your strength."

As we eat, he shares the mundane details of the business meeting he had while he was away. Most of his words don't register, as I'm more focused on his hand roaming over my body. It's as alluring as it is repulsive. His fingers and hands eliciting a response I desperately wish they wouldn't.

Wishing he would both remove his hands from me and finally touch the one place he hasn't.

"I can smell how fucking wet you are for me." He finishes the last of his dinner while I have barely managed to place a dent into mine. "Be honest. Does it upset you to know how much you actually enjoy my hands on you?"

"Yes," I answer hesitantly, unsure if he is baiting me.

"I appreciate your honesty." His hand glides up my inner thigh until his fingers slide into the satin shorts, just shy of my pussy. He rubs along the tender flesh at the crease of my upper thigh as he groans against my neck, "Does it make that tight little cunt of yours needy for me?"

"Yes." I'm disgusted at my own answer.

"What would my good little pet be willing to do to get that need taken care of?"

Anything...

CHAPTER FIFTEEN

GRANT

Sliding the robe from her shoulder, I kiss down the side of her neck before sinking my teeth into her shoulder causing her to yelp in pain. Kissing over the tender, bruising flesh, my lips vibrate against her skin. "Upstairs, kitten. It's time to play."

Around her, I have the fucking virility of a teenager. My cock ready at the mere thought of wrapping my ropes around her or slipping inside of her.

Obediently, she stands from my lap and waits for me to stand. I lead her to the room beside mine before removing the leash.

"Tell me." My hand slides over the curvature of her ass, "Have you ever taken a cock in your perfect little ass before?"

"No," she gulps as her eyes widen.

"Relax, kitten. I'm not a monster," I smirk as I lift a small metal plug from the shelf before us. "I'll work you up to it."

Besides, I'd fucking destroy her virgin ass for good if I didn't prep her first.

"Shorts off," I command while slathering lube over the plug. "And bend over the back of the couch for me."

Her eyes roam the other contents of the room and settle on a few sadistic impact toys I keep on hand for particular company before she complies with my demand. Bending slightly at the waist, she places her forearms on the back of the couch, exposing her ass.

"Spread your legs." I nudge them with my free hand as I kneel behind her. My lips roam over the skin of her ass while I spread her cheeks. "Has anyone ever licked this tight little virgin hole before?"

"No." She quickly exhales, her tone clearly declaring her repulsion to the idea.

"Oh, kitten, I'm going to enjoy changing your mind," I lick firmly over the puckered hole before teasing my tongue around it. The tip of my tongue swirls in repeated circles and firm long licks with the length of my tongue. Her breathy whimpers progress to moans as I press the tip of my tongue inside her. Instead of retreating from my touch, she pushes back for more.

After one more firm swipe of my tongue, I replace it with the amply lubricated plug in my hand. Gliding it around the tight eager hole and teasing her with the narrow tip. She groans as I work more of the plug into her.

"Your ass is so fucking eager." I twirl the plug in my hand as I press it all inside of her. Moving it slowly, I gingerly fuck her with the small plug.

"Fuck." Her thighs tremble as the toy in her ass works her toward the edge.

"Fuck, kitten." I press the plug into her, and it settles into place. "If this little toy is enough to make you come, you're going to love taking my fucking cock."

I stand behind her and spin her to face me, only to find the all too familiar pained look of denial written across her face.

"Are you afraid I'm going to edge you?" I question, and her eyes immediately give her answer. "Quite the opposite. You will come plenty tonight. I'm leaving the plug in, but the first time you come from getting your ass fucked it's not going to be from a small metal plug."

Grabbing a few bundles of jute and a wand, I lead her to the front of the couch. Taking a seat and placing the items beside me, I keep one bundle of rope in my hands. Making a loop, I affix it to the head of the wand with a square knot. Spreading the lips of Abigail's cunt, I nestle the wand firmly against her clit and use her hand to hold it in place. Circling the rope around her waist through the loop on the wand, I secure it to her clit.

Lifting the additional rope from the couch, I bind the body of the wand to her upper leg before working the ropes down her thighs to her knees. Using the final piece of jute, I bind her wrists together with ample slack between them. When I finish my ties, the wand is firmly pressed against her clit and wedged between her tightly bound thighs.

Standing from the couch, I circle my well-bound masterpiece as I slowly remove my clothes.

Fucking perfection.

Stroking my cock as I step behind her, I snake my arm around her waist. Retaking my seat on the couch, I pull her down onto my lap. Sliding my cock into her slick cunt as she sits, she lets out a groan of pleasure.

"Does my kitten like the fullness of all her holes being stuffed? Maybe one day I'll let you enjoy taking two cocks at once."

Or maybe even three.

She doesn't answer, but I hear her breathing begin to rapidly increase.

"Do you think it's too much? That you wouldn't be able to handle being fucked in both your tight little holes?"

"Yes," she whimpers.

"You'd be surprised what you can handle." I reach between her thighs, flip the wand to the lowest setting and her cunt immediately clenches around my cock. "You're going to sit nice and still on my lap with my cock nestled deep inside of you. The wand between your thighs forcing you to come for me over and over again."

Her chest heaves, and whimpers blow from her lips as the buzzing of the wand vibrates against her.

"We aren't going to stop until you're coming so fucking hard that your cunt quivers and clenches so tightly around my cock it makes me come inside you."

CHAPTER SIXTEEN

ABIGAIL

Grant's arms wrap around my waist, and his hands firmly grip each of my wrists. As he pulls each toward his sides, the slack rope between my hands stretches tight across my hips and pins me in place.

I feel so fucking full...

He is unwaveringly still inside of me as the vibrations of the wand cause my thighs to begin to convulse. Chewing at my bottom lip, I try to stifle my moans and fight giving him what he wants.

"Just do as he says, honey. It'll be for the best."

He releases my hand long enough to press a button on the toy strapped between my thighs, and I have no choice. The vibrations increase, and I cry out as the orgasm shoots through me. My thighs clench tighter together, and I shake on his lap as though the vibrations on my clit are making their way through my whole body.

"You feel so fucking good when that tight little cunt of yours comes around my cock." His lips rub against my ear as he whispers.

"Please," I beg, my hips and thighs still shaking from the relentless vibrations.

"Are you begging for more?" His voice is devilish as he increases the speed yet again.

My hips buck on his lap, trying to retreat from the blissfully painful vibrations. Each jolt of my body slides me along his length.

The plug...

...his massive cock...

...the vibrations shooting straight to my core.

Screaming in both pain and pleasure, my thighs flex so hard when I come again that I slide over the entirety of his length buried inside of me.

"Fuck," he snarls against my neck. His hands pull firmly at my wrists, digging the rope into my skin as he pulls me back down until he is buried to the hilt before increasing the speed yet again.

Every muscle in my body spasms as the wand continues its ruthless vibrations on my clit. The rope running over my hips digs through my flesh as my body writhes violently on his lap. Pulling fervently against all the ropes, grinding vigorously over his length as I futilely try to shake the wand forcing the unrelenting orgasms from me.

As I am almost having whole body spasms from the vibrations, Grant groans beneath me, "Fuck, kitten. I can't take it anymore."

Grabbing my hips, he attempts to hold my thrashing body in place as he savagely thrusts himself up into me. He comes with a roar, his rigid cock twitching inside me as he claims me yet again.

He switches off the wand and my fatigued body falls limp against him. My head lulls on his shoulder as I attempt to catch my breath. Every inch of me is painfully satiated.

And I fucking hate him for it.

Nearly as much as I hate myself for finding the faintest of enjoyment in it.

His fingers rub over my thighs as he works to undo each of the knots. The ropes fall to the floor beneath me, and his fingers linger over the constricting marks they left on my skin.

"You're a fucking masterpiece." He continues to trace my dimpled flesh. His touch is soft and soothing.

Grotesquely enjoyable.

My breaths are still deep and labored, and I fight against the heaviness of my eyelids as I feel Grant slowly going soft inside of me.

"Don't fight it, kitten." His knuckles dust over the side of my face as his lips press to my temple. "I'll take care of you, my pet."

As much as I don't want to listen, every bit of me is too tired to fight it.

———

Rolling over, his hand slides over my hip and onto my stomach as he sleepily groans, "Where are you going?"

Pulling me to him until my ass nests against his hips, he bends his legs behind mine until I am firmly spooned against his body. Holding me tightly to him, he nuzzles his face against the back of my neck. His slow deep breaths tickle as they blow against my skin.

My eyes closed and as I try to fall back to sleep, I meanderingly run my fingers over his arm steadfastly wrapped around my body.

His embrace is firm but so comforting.

It feels like...home.

Our skin already firmly pressed together; I push harder into his embrace. Needing the comfort he's giving me.

His lips kiss against my neck and I feel him beginning to grow hard against my ass. Toying with him, I wiggle my ass until I am tightly wedged against his hips.

He continues to kiss and suck at my neck, and I groan with need for him.

God, he feels so good.

"You wouldn't believe the dream I had, Garr." I hold his arm tighter against me as he continues to tease my neck.

He shifts his hips and I feel his tip resting against my pussy. He tightens his embrace, slowly sliding himself inside me as he whispers in my ear, "That wasn't a dream, kitten."

CHAPTER SEVENTEEN

GRANT

Abigail hasn't been here long, just a couple of weeks, but she is unlike any of the others. None of them have so willingly submitted to each of my desires. Or so eagerly followed my commands.

She enjoys being under my control.

She was fucking made to be my pet.

Curled into a ball beside me, she rests with her head on my thigh as I aimlessly stroke her soft blonde hair while I finalize some programming on my laptop. The unexpected ring of the doorbell draws me from both my work and my kitten.

"Be a good little kitten," I address her as I stand from the couch and give her a knowing nod.

"Yes, sir," she responds as she gets comfortable on the couch.

I catch a glimpse of a police cruiser parked out front as I pass a window.

Nothing ruins my day like this asshole.

"Detective Michales," I greet my unwanted guest when I open the door.

"Mr. Geyer." He tips his ridiculous fedora.

"I am assuming this isn't a social call." My tone is riddled with my disdain for him.

I mean, he could put me on death row if he didn't completely suck at his job.

"It's not," he responds flatly. "I'm here in regard to Mia Dillon."

"We've been through this more than once. If you want to speak with me regarding any of your witch hunt bullshit, you call my attorney."

"One of your cars was seen pulling from her property a couple weeks ago," he continues.

"Maybe I wasn't quite clear. I don't have any plans to tell you what the weather is doing or the time of day without my lawyer present. Now, I would appreciate it if you let yourself off my property the same way you managed to help yourself onto it." I push the door shut before he has a moment to say another word.

Walking past the window, I watch Detective Michales's eyes scan over the front of my estate as he leisurely meanders back to his car.

Continuing to watch him from the concealment of the curtains, I pull out my phone and text the group.

> Detective Asshole is on the hunt again

SAMUEL

Fuck that guy

EDMUND

Shut the fuck up kid. This is because of your carelessness.

LIZ

Maybe we should cancel tomorrow night

WILL

I can take care of the problem

SAMUEL

Kill the fucking pig

Stupid fucking kid. You're the problem he would be taking care of.

EDMUND

Party is on.

I got rid of Chloe a few weeks ago, and if I don't stick my dick in something soon...
Let's just say I may be liable to finally take Liz up on her offer

WILL

Keep the party on, I don't want his dick anywhere near me

LIZ

I keep telling you both, it's just a matter of time.

> Keep your dick in your pants until tomorrow night Samuel.

SAMUEL

No promises

LIZ

It'll be worth it.

I found the perfect fully expendable date for you.

> No one talks to the asshole.

EDMUND

Looking forward to finally meeting your new plaything.

I should have never sent him her photo.

He's been dying to fuck her ever since, and I refuse to let him mar her perfect skin.

LIZ

After the photo Eddie shared, I'd love to watch Will fuck her.

> You can't all fuck her.

WILL

But that means some of us can...

> I'll see you all tomorrow night.

Heading back to the living room where I left Abigail, I contemplate who I would most enjoy sharing her with tomorrow night.

And surprisingly, who she would most enjoy being fucked by.

Stepping into the living room, I am surprised to find Abigail no longer on the couch.

"Kitten?" I call out a moment before I hear her heels click on the hardwood floor behind me. Turning to find a glass of water in her hand, I praise her, "Look at you, drinking your water without even being told."

A faint smile of pride spreads across her face as she finishes the last of it. Taking the water from her, I cross the room. My eyes roam over every inch of her body and retake my seat on the couch. Those black heels, her toned calves, thick thighs, the curves of her hips being hugged by the white silk of her La Perla briefs, and her pert nipples poking against the silk of her matching camisole. But most of all, those green eyes, slightly shrouded by the hair hanging over her face, as she stares back at me.

"On your knees, kitten." My words slow and gravelly. Without dropping her gaze from mine, she lowers herself to follow my commands. "Crawl to me."

On all fours, with her eyes locked on mine, she slowly crosses the room. Her delicious ass sways slowly beyond the dipped arch in her back as she makes her way toward me.

"I still have work to finish, but I need to be inside you, kitten. Come wrap those lips of yours around my cock."

Spreading my knees as she reaches me, she settles herself between my feet and unzips my pants. Her soft hand wraps around my cock, and I can't stifle my groan. Pulling my cock out, she sweeps her tongue around my tip and slides her lips down my shaft.

Fuck, she feels good.

CHAPTER EIGHTEEN

ABIGAIL

Taking Grant into my mouth, I swallow his length. Taking him the way he told me he likes.

"I said I have work to do, kitten." He gently nudges my head to his thigh and holds my head still. Tenderly rubbing his fingers along my jaw and cheek, he beams down at me with a look of pride. "Hold my cock and be still while I finish up."

As though I don't currently have him in my mouth, he grabs his laptop and returns to his work. After a few minutes, I teasingly swirl tongue around his tip.

"I said be still, kitten," he snarls as his fingers roughly fist my hair. Immediately stilling my tongue, I rest my head back against his thigh and do as he commanded.

He really does just want me to hold him in my mouth.

His fingers linger in my hair as he continues to work, occasionally petting me. It feels like it has been an eternity, my cheeks beginning to hurt from the 'O' wrapped around his shaft.

"Such a good little pet." His knuckles drag slowly against my sore jaw. "Patiently waiting for me to take your throat."

As much as I don't want them to, his words shoot straight to my pussy.

Just like they always do.

Same as his touch.

I want to hate it. I want to hate him, but the neediness between my thighs continues to betray me time and time again.

"You'd like that, wouldn't you, kitten?" he questions as he closes his laptop and places it beside him on the couch.

Bending forward, his hand slides down my spine and dips beneath the silk of my panties. His fingers gently push against the flared base of the plug he placed inside me this morning, and I can't help but groan around him in my mouth.

"After I fuck your throat," he groans as he begins to grow hard in my mouth. "I'm going to finally fuck this tight little ass of yours."

Sitting up, his hands slip into the hair on either side of my head. He uses the leverage to slowly slide me over his length. The moment he is fully hard, he lifts until I'm circling his tip. His fingers tighten in the hair at the back of my head and forcefully shoves my head until my lips are pressed against his pelvis.

"Fuck," he groans, repeatedly sliding me over the entirety of him. "How eager you are to have me buried inside you. Swallowing my cock like you can't get enough."

Sliding me off him, he tips my head until my eyes meet his. He stares deep into them; his voice soft when he speaks, "Upstairs, kitten. Take off the panties and get on the bed. I want you comfortable when I take that virgin ass."

Swallowing hard, I place my hands on his thighs to lift myself from between his knees. As I rise, his fingers dust along the silk covering my pussy. I quiver in response, and it elicits a devilish smirk from him. He doesn't say a word. He merely gestures toward the door.

As someone who has always been appalled by the thought of a dick in my ass, it isn't lost on me how wet I am right now. Grant has been teasing me with increasingly larger plugs almost daily for two weeks.

And I like them...

Walking into the bedroom, I do exactly as I was told. I remove my panties and sit on the edge of the bed. A moment later, Grant steps into the doorway. I can't help but scan over his now-naked body. For a man his age, his physique is impeccable—broad shoulders, muscular arms, rippled abs. Continuing down his body, my eyes stop on his beautiful dick.

Yes, it's beautiful...

Fully erect and resting against his stomach, every inch of his thick length on display.

And it looks nearly as good as it feels.

Fuck, Abby...

Grant crosses the room, and I notice he is holding a bullet vibrator and a bottle of lube. Stepping between my thighs, he places the vibe in my hand as he gently instructs, "Lie back, kitten and put your feet on the bed."

Laying back and on display for him, he begins to tease at the toy in my ass, as he growls, "Your cunt is dripping, and I've barely fucking touched you."

His thumb rubs teasingly overly my clit while he slowly works the plug in and out of my ass. My chest heaves as he continues, enjoying every second of it. He pulls it from me, and I groan at the sudden feeling of emptiness.

"Use it on your clit." He grabs my hand with the vibe and pulls it between my thighs. "It'll help keep you relaxed."

I whimper at the light vibrations, watching as Grant slathers himself with lube. Gripping his base, he presses the thick head against me, and I can't help but to clench with her nerves.

"Relax, kitten." He rubs his tip around the hole. "You can take me."

He presses harder against me, and I breathe in deeply, trying desperately to stay relaxed. He carefully presses his tip inside before stilling, "I intend to make sure you enjoy this. I want to leave you begging for my cock in your ass again. And soon."

CHAPTER NINETEEN

GRANT

Rubbing the vibe over her clit and breathing slowly, Abigail relaxes enough that I'm able to press inside of her tight virgin ass.

And fuck is it tight.

"Eyes on me, kitten," I groan, holding her hips as I inch inside her. "I don't want you to miss a second of me claiming your ass."

Her eyes bore into mine, she chews her lower lip and whimpers as I slowly bury myself in her to the hilt. Tentatively working myself in and out of her, ensuring not to hurt her, I continue to stretch her ass until it's eagerly accepting my cock. As her body adjusts to my size, I begin to pick up speed. Both of us moan with each tender thrust.

"Fuck, kitten." I bury myself deep inside her. Sliding my hands under her lower back, I lift her enough to position us both on the bed. I settle on top of her, and work myself in and out of her ass as I kiss along her neck. Suckling along her collarbone, I mark yet another inch of her as mine.

Her hands knead against the flexing muscles of my back with each stroke, and her mewls become increasingly louder.

"Are you going to come for me?" I whisper in her ear.

"Yes," she moans as her legs wrap around my waist, only urging me to take her harder. Driving my cock into her, I kiss her lips and swallow the screams of her orgasm.

Continuing to thrust into her, my lips dust over hers, and I groan, "Does my kitten like my cock in her ass?"

"Yes, sir." She squeezes her legs and pulls me deeper.

"Tell me." I kiss her hard, leaving us both breathless when I pull away.

"You feel so good...and your massive cock. I feel so fucking full...it's almost too much," she breathlessly pants as I continue to fuck her.

"You can take more." I plunge into her. "You'd look so fucking gorgeous with a cock buried in your ass and another in your cunt."

Her eyes widen at my words, but the quick thrusts of my cock leave her unable to speak. All that comes from her mouth is repeated screams as she comes for me again.

The screams of pleasure and her ass squeezing around my cock do me in. Thrusting a final time, I drive into the hilt with a roar as I spill my cum deep inside her ass.

"You're mine, kitten." My words sputtered by my heavy breaths as I nearly crumple on top of her. Cupping the side of her face, my lips brush over hers before I lightly press my tongue between them. They part for me willingly, and my tongue intertwines with hers. Pulling back with her lip between my teeth, I nip at it gently before letting go.

"Yours…" she groans as I pull my cock from her ass.

Leaving her on the bed, I retreat to the adjoining bathroom to grab a damp washcloth to clean her up.

"Sir?" she questions as I gently clean her.

"Yes, kitten?" I clean myself and toss the cloth to the floor before climbing back into bed with her.

"Did you mean it?"

"Mean what?"

"What you said about me taking two men at once." Her words are soft and hesitant.

"Yes," I respond as I swipe the hair from her face. She doesn't reply, but I can see the nervous look in her eyes.

"You'll love the feeling of two sets of hands and lips all over your perfect body. We'll start slow, tomorrow night," I pull her close and pepper kisses against her forehead.

"Tomorrow, sir?" I hear the trepidation in her voice.

"I enjoy letting others play with my pets. I want to share you, and you're going to eagerly take their cocks like you take mine. Like the good little pet you are." I press my lips firmly to her temple. "You want to be a good little pet for me, don't you?"

"Yes, sir." She swallows hard.

"Even when I share you, you belong to me. You will only ever belong to me." I climb from the bed and walk down the hall. Opening a drawer under the candles for wax play, I pull out a lighter.

Flicking the flint until it lights, I hold the flame over the ring on my finger as I return to the bedroom. The band around my finger warms as I continue to hold the flame over the ornate 'G' engraved on the face of my ring.

"You will only ever be mine, kitten." I breathe through the heat burning around my finger. "Now spread those thighs for me so we can ensure everyone else knows it too."

She audibly gulps as she follows my command. Still heating the face of the band, I climb between her thighs. Dropping the lighter, I use my free hand to forcibly hold her knee to the bed. Bracing my forearm over her hip, my tone gravelly when I say, "Take a deep breath, this is going to hurt."

As she sucks in air I press the ring into her upper thigh beside her sweet cunt, searing her flesh. Her deep breath immediately hisses painfully back over her lips. Pulling back, her flesh is marked with a bright red square with my initial centered in it.

"Mine, kitten." I kiss beside the tender skin as I release my firm grip on her leg. "For the rest of your life."

CHAPTER TWENTY

ABIGAIL

Finishing my make-up and curling my hair as Grant requested, I can't stop thinking about how this is the longest he has gone without touching me in all the time I've been here.

And how I don't like it.

Stepping from the bathroom, wearing only a towel, I find Grant fully dressed in one of his many well-tailored suits. Arms crossed, his eyes are fixated on the green and gold painting I gifted him upon my arrival.

He stares at that painting nearly as much as he stares at me.

When I make my way across the room, I find that he has laid my attire for the evening on the bed—a sleek navy dress, nude thigh highs, and a sheer black thong.

Lifting the thong from the bed draws Grant's attention, and he promptly says, "Allow me."

His fingers tug at the towel, and it falls to the ground at my feet as he takes the thong from my hand. Kneeling before me, he positions the panties for me to step into them. Once they're around my ankles, he drags them up my legs and over my hips before placing a soft kiss over the still tender flesh he burned his mark into last night.

"Sit." He gestures to the bed as he grabs one of the nylon stockings from his position on the floor. Bunching the opening toward the tip, he slips it over my toes before resting my foot on his chest. At the same time as he stares into my eyes, his fingers slide to my upper thighs as he positions the lacy garter. The lustful look in his eyes grows, and he repeats the process for the other stocking.

How in the hell is getting dressed hotter than having your clothes ripped off?

Pulling the dress from the bed, he slips it up my legs before helping me stand. As he slides it up my body, I slip my arms into the sheer billowed sleeves. He arranges it over my shoulders, and dusts my hair out of the way to tie the strings of the dress at the nape of my neck. His lips kissing above the knot, he takes advantage of the open back of the dress and glides his knuckles down my spine.

"You are fucking gorgeous, kitten." He holds my back to his chest as he stares at the two of us in the mirror. "I'm almost tempted to keep you here for myself tonight."

Please...

After slipping the heels on my feet, he leads me downstairs and to the front door. He turns the knob to open it, and ushers me through it and down the steps to the waiting car.

I've passed this door hundreds of times in the past two weeks, but not once have I ever checked to see if it was unlocked.

Grant opens the passenger door of the sleek, black sports car and holds my hand to help me into the passenger seat. Kissing my knuckles, he releases my hand and shuts the door. Quickly, he rounds the car and climbs into the driver's seat. After putting the car into gear, his hand is immediately on my knee and sliding up my inner thigh.

His grip unwaveringly firm, he speeds down winding country roads. When we finally come to a stop, it is in front of a gate equally as ornate as the one in front of his home. Releasing me from his grip, he pulls a card from his pocket and swipes it over a box just beyond his car window. The gate slowly draws open, and he pulls through.

Taking the long drive at the same speed as the roads before it, I try to determine just how far back we are from the road.

Far...

Clearing the trees, we pull before a massive estate with a few cars parked before it.

Either we are early, or this is a small party.

Grant parks the car and walks around to open my door. Helping me from the car, he slips my hand into the crook of his arm. The two of us walking into this place as though I am his date, not his pet.

The door opens when we reach it, and a well-dressed man is waiting on the other side with a tray containing two drinks.

"Mr. Geyer." He dips his head. "Your Gibson Martini and a Tennessee Mule for the lady."

My eyes dart to Grant as he retrieves the drink for me.

He remembered my drink?

"You get just one, kitten. No one wants a sloppy fuck. Understood?" His words feel cold as he places the copper cup in my hands.

For every shred of evidence I get that I'm more than just a plaything to him, it feels as though I get two more to recant it.

Threading my arm back into his, I follow his lead down the hall. We pass a room with a few beautiful women waiting anxiously on a couch. My eyes linger on them for a moment as I wonder why I'm not left to wait there with them.

Reaching the door at the end of the hall, Grant pauses before opening it. Turning to me, he firmly grips my chin and pulls my eyes up to his. His voice is quiet and deep when he speaks, "Obedient little pets do what is asked of them to please their owners. You know what I want from you. Are you going to be a good little kitten for me tonight?"

The idea of being fucked by two men at once intrigues me.

But more than anything I wish that it were happening on entirely different terms.

My terms.

Swallowing hard, I push out a quiet, "Yes, sir."

"That's a good girl." He places a soft kiss on my lips before releasing my chin.

CHAPTER TWENTY-ONE

DETECTIVE MICHALES

When I first joined the police force of Adelaide Cove, this place was the type of perfect little town where television shows took place. The type of quiet oceanfront town where people slept with their doors open. For years, the most exciting things that happened around here were petty shoplifting from bored kids and an occasional bar fight from the summer tourists.

Things began to change when those tourists slowly started to move here, turning Adelaide Cove into their full-time residence. Now the picturesque town I love has become a cesspool of filth and crime. The most frequent of which are women disappearing and claims of sexual assault.

I hate what this fucking town has become.

...and the rich entitled assholes and the expensive as hell attorneys they all have on retainer.

Everything started with the sudden disappearance of four women—Madeline O'Rourk, Cameryn Weathers, Paisley Allen, and Chloe Wilson. Their missing persons reports rolled in days to weeks apart, but they all had one thing in common. Every last one of them had told someone close to them they were going to some life-changing event.

And poof. Each of them was gone without a trace.

All of them except Paisley. A now-recanted eye-witness report was given about two months after her disappearance was reported with information stating she was seen at the home of Edmund Parker.

In the days it took to convince a judge to sign a search warrant for his home, she was gone.

Just like the rest of them.

Unable to get the rest of the department to look past their prestigious facades and continuous generous donations to our little town, I'm the joke of an officer who refuses to let this go.

They've become my obsession, slowly ruining my life. My career. My marriage. My relationships with my children. All of them dwindling from existence like the women of this town.

The moment Mia Dillon came forward to press assault charges against Samuel Millington, I thought I finally had my in. The small sliver of evidence that was going to cause their perfect little worlds to implode. But once again, they were two steps ahead of me. Leaving everything she owned behind, Mia disappeared with her son in the middle of the night.

Not a trace, just like the rest of them.

Unable to let this one go, I've been attached to Samuel Millington almost twenty-four hours a day for the past couple of weeks. Excluding the barrage of willing women passing through his gates daily, nothing has happened that even remotely helps my case.

Parked down the block from the entrance to his estate, I'm about to fall asleep when I hear the motor of the gate kick on. He pulls through it, and I shield my face as he drives past my unmarked car.

Quickly flipping on my headlights, I slip the car into drive and make a U-turn. I keep my distance and follow a few car lengths behind him through town. Reaching the outskirts, I drop back further when he begins to travel down desolate country roads.

I'm going to fucking lose him...

Accelerating and risking being seen, I round a turn revealing a vacant straightaway.

"Fuck!" I slam my fist against the steering wheel as I accelerate. Speeding past it, I almost miss the iron gates tucked into the tree line. They are closing, and I can faintly see the taillights of his sports car in the distance.

Continuing several yards past the entrance, I park my car between the trees on the opposite side of the road before cutting the engine and turning off the lights.

I consider grabbing the handle to open the car door, but hesitate when I see headlights rounding the turn. Momentarily blinded by them, I immediately recognize the face behind the steering wheel—Edmund Parker. He no more than passes through the gate when another car approaches—William Cattaneo and Elizabeth Beaufort.

Son of a fucking bitch.

Stepping from the car, I immediately duck behind it when I hear a roaring engine in the distance. A sleek, black Bugatti squeals to a stop at the gate—Grant fucking Geyer.

I hit the fucking lottery.

Sprinting toward the gate as he pulls through, I manage to slip inside just before it closes. Quickly pulling a small flashlight from my pocket I watch as Geyer's taillights disappear in the distance. I flip on the light and begin walking in the direction that they disappeared.

Nearly an hour has passed by the time I reach the clearing, revealing a massive estate. The four sports cars are the only things parked out front. Sneaking along the perimeter, I see no evidence of cameras or security.

Keeping low, I cross the yard and press my back against the exterior of the home. I carefully slink along it, peering into each of the windows that I pass, which reveal luxurious vacant rooms.

The faint sound of a woman's screams draws my attention and causes my ears to perk up. Drawing my gun, I increase the speed at which I make my way around the house. Two more screams, distinctly different, quickly have me begin running between the windows.

Looking in a window at the rear of the home, I find the source of the screams.

Fuck!

CHAPTER TWENTY-TWO

GRANT

Holding Abigail close, both for her comfort and mine, I lead her into the devil's lair where Edmund, Will, Liz, and Samuel are waiting for our arrival.

Samuel eyes over her, practically salivating. As though I can hear every deviant thought in his mind, I glare at him as a reminder of my recent visit to his home. He immediately diverts his lusty gaze when he sees me watching.

Of everyone in this room, the only chance he has of laying a finger on Abigail is going to be over my cold, dead body.

Edmund approaches from the bar, and Abigail jumps as his fingers run down her bare spine. Squeezing her hip I whisper in her ear, "Mine, kitten."

"You're fucking gorgeous." He leans close to her. "Please tell me every inch of her skin is this fucking glorious."

"It is." I raise a knowing eyebrow. "But there is no way in hell you're going to leave a single mark on it."

Sitting on William's lap, Liz presses a kiss to William's cheek before crossing the room to us. She places her hand on the small of Abigail's back and the other on my chest and leans into us both, speaking with a slightly excitable tone, "Since Samuel is clearly out of the running, and my dear friend Eddie is banned from whipping her flawless skin, does that mean William and I are going to have the pleasure of your entertainment this evening? It's been far too long since I've been witness to that magical cock of yours."

"Liz," Will snarls from his seat.

"What?" She shrugs. "You've seen it. That big, beautiful cock deserves to be marveled at."

Quickly crossing the room, Will wraps his fingers around Liz's throat and pulls her from the two of us. His deep whisper in her ear is clearly audible to the rest of us. "You may enjoy being degraded, but I do not. If you want to come on anyone's cock tonight, I suggest you cut the shit."

"Yes, baby," she smirks, Will just walked right into what she wanted.

We all know as punishment he'll be extra cruel to her this evening.

"Unlike Samuel, I'm not into women who scream and fight back. Is your new little plaything going to be a willing participant this evening?" The contention in Will's voice toward Samuel is quite apparent.

"Do you need her to prove it to you?" My hand rubs over Abigail's hip.

Still firmly holding Liz's neck, Will's eyes roll over Abigail's body as he says, "She can show Liz."

"Show Liz what a good little pet you are, kitten." I place a soft kiss on her temple.

Her eyes linger on mine for a moment, and her chest heaves as she steps toward Liz. Their lips dust for a moment before Liz licks between Abigail's lips. I watch as they willingly part to accept Liz's tongue; Abigail's hands slide around her waist to pull her closer as their kiss becomes increasingly more passionate. Their tongues wrestle and their hands roam each other's bodies until both of them are panting into each other's mouths.

"Knowing how much she's enjoying you right now, I think my baby girl is going to love watching me fuck you." Will pulls Liz backward and breaks their kiss. Spinning her around, he claims her mouth as she rubs herself against the cock tenting against the front of his pants.

"Two million," Liz pants as she pulls back from Will. "Eddie, love, you get Will's and Grant's too."

Edmund's face lights up at bloody foursome he's about to have, and Samuel huffs, "What the fuck, he gets both of them?"

"Maybe when you learn to behave outside of this house, we'll treat you a little better, kid," Edmund snarks before practically skipping from the room to go collect his women.

"Get the fuck out, Samuel," Liz demands as her hand rubs under her skirt between her thighs. "Watching these two fuck her is going to be my private show."

"Then you better remove your hand from that dirty cunt between your legs," Will snarls. "Shut the fuck up and take a seat in the corner where you fucking belong."

Liz's thighs clench as she walks to the chair opposing the couch. She crosses her legs at the thigh and continues to grind them together for relief.

"You liked kissing her, didn't you?" I whisper in Abigail's ear as I kiss down her neck.

"Yes," she whispers as I tug at the strings securing the dress behind her shoulders.

"Be a good little pet, and maybe next time I'll get you something pretty to play with. Do you think you would like that, kitten?"

"Yes, sir," she hesitantly moans as I pull the dress down her arms and it falls to the floor as Will's lips join mine on her neck.

"Look at this perfectly round ass." Will grinds against her. "I can't wait to sink my cock into it."

"Cunt or mouth," I snarl, surprising even myself. "Her ass is mine. And it will only ever be mine."

My cock will be the only one to have had the pleasure of enjoying that tight little hole.

Abigail mouths the words *thank you*, as Will kisses along her shoulder and spins her between us. Kneeling before her, he pulls her sheer thong to the side and groans at the sight of her shaved cunt.

Pressing his forehead to her stomach, his head lolls as he breathes her in. "You sweet cunt smells so fucking good. I want to bury my face in."

"On the couch and spread those legs, kitten," I groan.

My groan only partially from my arousal, but more from knowing Will is about to dip his tongue into my cunt.

CHAPTER TWENTY-THREE

ABIGAIL

Taking a slow couple steps backward, William never releases my panties as he crawls across the floor with his face mere inches from my pussy. As I sit, he pushes my knees apart, and settles between my feet.

Gripping my ass with one hand, he drags me to the edge of the couch, "Such a perfect, pink pussy. I don't even need to put my cock in it to see how fucking tight it is. Are you more excited for my tongue or cock, Abigail?"

"Eyes on me, kitten." Grant grips my chin, tipping it toward him as he sits beside me on the couch. William licks over my clit and my eyes clamp shut as I swallow hard. Breathing deeply, I fight the urge to shove him away from me. Grant repeats himself, his voice firm yet reassuring, "I said, eyes on me."

Grant slips his thumb into my mouth, and I eagerly suck at it as I stare into the blue pools of his eyes. "That's it. Keep them on me."

The tongue between my thighs continues to lap at me, but I'm so fixated on Grant that I almost forget it's connected to William.

Cupping the sides of my face, Grant crashes his lips into mine. Parting my lips, he plunges his tongue into my mouth and aggressively reminds me that I belong to him. Squeezing at his shoulders, I moan into his mouth, needing so much more of him.

It's just me and Grant...

Continuing to kiss me, his hand slides over my heaving chest and down my bare stomach. Grazing past where William's tongue works diligently over my clit, Grant grips the tender flesh he marked last night as he growls against my lips, "Mine, kitten. Now be a good pet and come for me."

Staring into Grant's eyes I let go, clawing at his shoulders, breathless mewls blow over my lips as William's tongue sends me over the edge.

Coming for Grant...

...only for Grant.

"If I didn't need to be inside you this badly." William pulls his dick from his pants and climbs on the couch as he and Grant situate me on all fours. "I'd eat you out all night. That delicious cunt of yours is fucking addicting."

Keeping my gaze, Grant bends forward and kisses my lips before whispering in my ear, "Keep those eyes on me, just me, as you suck my cock."

Sitting back for a moment, he unzips his pants and pulls out his throbbing cock. He fists the base of his shaft as he returns to his knees and rubs the tip against my lips.

"Is this the magical cock you wanted to see?" he snarls at Liz. "Enjoy it, because it only goes inside my kitten."

Opening my mouth and staring up at him, I willingly take him to the base and allow him to slide me up and down his shaft slowly. Teasing over his length with my tongue, I watch as his brows furrow and feel William press himself inside me.

"This might be the tightest cunt I've ever fucked," William growls from behind me. "Liz's saggy used snatch doesn't even come close."

My eyes momentarily dart to Liz and she's writhing in the chair; his words only seem to encourage her need. Grant grips my chin and immediately draws my attention back to him. His upper lip continues to twitch as though he's fighting back a snarl.

Is he unhappy because I'm doing something wrong?

I maintain my pace, sucking him in deeply, and William drives into me from behind.

"This cunt is fucking perfect, baby girl. I can't fucking handle it," he snarls at Liz as his hands grip my hips. Beginning to thrust relentlessly into me, he grips my shoulder and growls, "I'm going to show you who owns this fucking pussy, Abigail."

"I do," Grant roars as he plunges down my throat. "Don't

even think about putting a drop of your cum inside of her."

William slows his thrusts behind me nearly to a halt as the mood in the room suddenly shifts.

What the fuck just happened?

"My kitten likes to be bathed in her cream," I groan as Grant pulls my mouth. My eyes dart between his and the hand he's using to violently fist his dick, when I feel William pull out of me as well.

Gripping my throat with his free hand, Grant pushes me back onto my heels. The two of them stand before me, their hands slide over their hard cocks as I stare at Grant. The eyes staring back at me look pained as he silently pumps his cum, which spurts across my breasts.

A moment later, William groans, and Grant diverts his eyes from me as William's warm cum splatters across my neck and on my breasts with Grant's. Their cum mixes as it drips down my breasts and runs down my stomach.

I suddenly feel so fucking dirty.

"You should've told me." William smears the cum running down my neck. "I would've saved up for her."

"Fuck," Liz pants from the corner as her ass grinds against the chair.

"You did so good." William crosses the room to her and plunges two of his salty fingers into her mouth. "Do you want to ride my tongue or my hand until I'm ready to put my cock inside you?"

Pulling the fingers from her mouth, she shoves them under her skirt, and her head falls back when he doesn't hesitate to press inside her.

Without placing a momentary glance in my direction, Grant has tucked himself back into his pants and removed his jacket.

Tossing it on the couch beside me, he snarls, "Put it on. Leave your stuff. We're going."

What did I do wrong?

Tears well in my eyes as I slide my arms into his oversized jacket. Wrapping it snuggly around my cum-covered body, I quickly follow behind him down the hall and to the front door.

CHAPTER TWENTY-FOUR

GRANT

Fuck!

Storming outside, I hastily make my way to the car and pull open the passenger door.

"Get in the fucking car," I growl at Abigail who is just making her way down the stairs. She scuttles across the circular drive in her heels and drops into the passenger seat. When she is fully inside, I slam the door shut.

I mutter profanities to myself, and quickly make my way around the car. I climb into the driver's seat and slam my door as well before pushing the ignition. Roughly shifting into reverse, I pull from my spot and shift into drive. The tires grind against the asphalt before propelling the car forward.

Speeding down the drive, the gate has barely opened far enough for the car when I squeeze through it. Making a hard turn, Abigail grips the door handle as she gasps.

"Sir," she mumbles.

I can't fucking do this right now.

My nostrils flare as I continue to breathe through my seething anger. Roughly banking each turn down the windy country roads, I need to be as far away from there as possible right now.

I need to be home.

"Did I do something wrong?" She struggles to look at me as she timidly broaches her question.

"Not now," I sneer. "I can't fucking talk to you about this right now."

Reaching town, I slightly lower my speed, but continue my way toward my estate at well above the posted speed limit.

"Sir?" Her voice is pained, and I don't have to look at her to know that tears are welling in her eyes.

Ignoring her, I continue my way through the streets that are nearly vacant at this hour.

"Grant?" I can hear the tremble of her lips as she speaks my name for the first time in weeks.

It feels like a knife to my fucking cold, black heart.

"I said, not now," I yell the words, needing her to stop.

Pulling through the gate of my estate, I pull to a stop at the front door. My fingers flex around the steering wheel and I practically grunt the words, "Upstairs, now."

I faintly hear her mumble, "Okay," as she opens her own car door. Leaving her to trail behind, I storm upstairs to the master bathroom and turn the water in the shower. By the time she reaches the room, steam is beginning to billow from the stall.

"Strip and get in the fucking shower." The words spit through my gritted teeth.

Trembling before me, I watch a tear roll down her cheek as she kicks off her heels and drops my suit jacket to the floor. Removing her panties, she proceeds to push off each of the nylon stockings. Her hands awkwardly cover her breasts as she stands naked before me.

"In the shower," I growl. "Scrub every fucking trace of him from your skin."

I hate that he spread his cum across her skin, but not nearly as much as I hate knowing that he had his cock inside of her.

Inside of what is mine.

Pets and various playthings have made their way through my home throughout the years. Not once have I had a moment of hesitation with regard to sharing them with anyone. Least of all William, Liz or Edmund. I've shared countless, faceless women with them over the years. This definitely wasn't the first time I've played with Liz's cuckcake of the night.

But this was different...

I felt it the moment Will put his lips on her skin. It only amplified when he mentioned his interest in claiming her perfect little ass hole.

My perfect little ass hole.

Keeping Abigail's focus on me wasn't entirely for her sake, it was just as much for mine. So I could attempt to negate the fact that he had his hands and mouth roaming her body. That he was going to place his cock inside what I had already claimed as mine.

When I watched him press himself inside of her, I fought the urge to shove him from her and bury my fist into his face. For having the gall to take what I had so eagerly presented to him.

Fuck...

Pacing in the bedroom, I strip from my clothes before returning to the bathroom. The water is beginning to run cold in the shower, yet Abigail continues to stand under the stream, scrubbing soap over her body. She scrubs viciously as though she, too, needs to remove all evidence of him from her.

Stepping into the lukewarm spray of the water, her bloodshot eyes stare up at me, her lower lip trembles as she asks, "Did I do something wrong?"

Not knowing how to answer, I continue to block her from the spray of the water that is still dropping in temperature.

"Please, sir," she pleads, and the pained look her eyes nearly breaks me.

Wiping the tears from her cheeks, my voice is soft when I finally respond, "I'm not mad at you, kitten. You did everything I asked of you."

CHAPTER TWENTY-FIVE

ABIGAIL

"I don't understand." My jaw trembles as I fight back the overwhelming urge to cry over disappointing him.

Droplets of icy water ricochet off Grant's body, chilling me when they hit my skin. Yet, he stands unwavering before me, taking the brunt of the frigid spray of the water.

"You were the perfect pet tonight, willfully following each of my commands. Doing exactly what I demanded of you." His voice still tender as he cups my face, his thumbs continue to wipe the trickling tears from my cheeks. "I am not the least bit upset with you."

"Then?"

"I said I'm not mad at you, kitten," he huffs the words.

Goosebumps begin to prickle over my skin as the little warmth from the steam of the previously hot water has been replaced with cool air. Freezing, I watch Grant's face and wait silently for him to continue.

"You're my pet. A fucking toy I paid for. A tight little hole for me to fuck as I desire and to pass around as I please." His tone flat as he speaks the words.

I know what I am to him...

...what he took me for...

...that I should harbor more vile hatred for him than any man that walks this earth.

Yet, hearing him say the words out loud breaks my fucking heart.

My lower lip quivers and my ability to hold back the stream of tears is lost. I sob silently as they begin to pour uncontrollably down my cheeks.

"Disposable when I tire of you. Completely fucking expendable. No one to miss you when you're left in an unmarked shallow grave..." His voice trails off.

I was right from the beginning...

I'm going to die here.

"That's all any of them were. That's all that you're supposed to be, kitten." He presses me backward until my back is flush against the freezing stone tiles of the shower before boxing me in with his body.

"His lips on your skin and watching him enjoy what belongs to me..." His jaw ticks as he clenches his teeth. "I may have offered you to him, but I could have fucking killed him for being inside you."

The back of his hand drags along my skin, which is nearly raw from scrubbing where William had smeared his vile cum over me.

"The thought of another man ever touching you again fills me with an indescribable rage. The devil in me willing to do the unspeakable." His hands slide down my sides until they're both resting on my hips. "Things that would make Satan himself question his morality...For my kitten."

Staring up at him, my voice strained when I ask, "Then why won't you look at me?"

"Because the moment I meet those green eyes of yours, I'm going to have to admit to myself that I might actually care about something—*someone*—for the first time in my life."

Closing my eyes, I relish in the feel of his hands roaming along my sides. I take a deep breath and reach my hand up to his jaw, and I whisper, "Sir..."

Please look at me.

Tell me I matter.

Lifting his eyes from my body, his gaze meets mine. My heart races and my chest heaves, yet I feel as though I am unable to breathe. The look in his eyes destroys me.

I feel whole and broken, all at once.

"This will never be a fairytale, kitten." His tone is gravelly and rough as his fingers rake over my hips. Firmly digging into the backs of my thighs, he wraps my legs around his waist as he drives himself into me.

I gasp at the sudden intrusion and squeeze my thighs against him. Wrapping my arms around his neck, I shiver when they rub over the cold skin on his back.

He's fucking freezing.

He carries me from the shower, using his grip on my thighs to slide me over his length. Reaching the bed, he spreads me across it before climbing between my thighs. When he aligns himself with my entrance, he hesitates to push back into me.

"There are no happily ever after's with the devil." His lips dust against mine, vibrating as he speaks as he presses the entirety of himself back into me

There is no magical movie moment.

My villain doesn't become a hero.

There is no Prince Charming.

No white knight.

No sweeping me off my feet and making love to me.

This isn't a fairytale.

Grant's fingers wrap around my throat, squeezing as he continues to thrust into me. Tightening his grip, he presses his lips to my ear before groaning, "You're going to take every last demanding inch of my cock like the good little pet you are. Your cunt is mine."

He fucks me hard and fast, the tight grip around my throat nearly cuts off my ability to breathe. My vision begins to blacken around the edges, and he slams into me. Fucking terrified that this is my end, my body explodes beneath him, his fingers clamping around my throat silence my screams.

"You're fucking mine," Grant roars as his hips spasm against me.

CHAPTER TWENTY-SIX

DETECTIVE MICHALES

Hooking my phone up to my laptop, I download the video I recorded last night. I have already rewatched it countless times, but the small screen of my phone just isn't enough.

Pressing play, the shaky, homemade porn begins streaming across the glossy screen. Edmund Parker having his way with three yet-to-be-named, young women. Although they are all in various types of bondage and restraints, the acts that I am watching are clearly completely consensual.

And that's the only reason I didn't intervene when I stumbled upon them last night.

Edmund pounds into a redhead. As he fucks her, her face is buried between the thighs of one of the other two women. Both of her arms are bound in leather cuffs behind her back, his hands wrapped around the chain between them as he fucks her from behind. He thrusts hard, causing her hair to fall over her shoulder. And at that point, I press pause on the video.

Grabbing some paper, I draw a rough sketch of the small, purple butterfly tattoo just below her shoulder before documenting its location. I resume the video, keeping my full focus on the redhead I don't concentrate on the strikes of leather hitting her back or the railing she is taking, but entirely on her.

Trying to find out all I can so that I can hopefully determine who she is.

About ten minutes later, she lifts her face, and I quickly press the pause button again. Taking a screenshot, I zoom and crop before printing out the photo for my records.

I reset the video and watch through to the end. I then do it again, resuming from the beginning to watch her again. And again, before I turn my gaze to the blonde she was servicing. I continuously loop the video on repeat, looking for more details, as though it is an obsession.

Because it is.

By the time I am done, I have photos printed of each of the women and a couple of additional descriptors for two of them. I grab all the papers, I shove them into a folder before heading over to the precinct.

While it may be too soon for missing person's reports to have been placed on them yet, I want this information at the front desk in the event someone does come forward. Making several copies, I distribute them throughout the office ensuring everyone knows the faces of these three women.

"Michales? Is there some sort of investigation into the porn industry the rest of us aren't aware of?" Callahan holds one of the photos in the air and he has a shit-eating grin sprawled across his face. The only screenshots I could grab of the second blonde all are obvious in pointing to what was transpiring.

"I've been telling all of you—"

"What the fuck Michales!" the chief yells as he walks into the office, snatching up the photographs as he makes his rounds, "My office. Now."

Trying not to tuck my tail between my legs, I follow him to the sound of the others mocking me like a child being sent to the principal's office.

Stepping into his office, he slams the door behind me and throws the evidence across his desk before taking a seat.

"I ask, you answer," he huffs. His eyes dart between me and the papers strewn across his desk. "Is this Edmund Parker?"

"Yes." I nod.

"For the love of Christ, tell me you downloaded it from some self-posting pornography website," he pauses. "Is that where it came from?"

"No, Chief," he shakes his head as I answer. "I was following Samuel Millington, and—"

"Shut the fuck up. Right now," he cuts me off and stands behind his desk. His palms flat on the splayed photos before him, his nostrils flare, visible even with his head hung low in defeat.

"You're a fucking detective," he snarls at me. "Not some vigilante bounty hunter. Evidence. Warrants. Laws. Fuck, Michales."

"Chief. I *know* they're all guilty as sin. Each of—"

"It doesn't matter what your gut says. It matters what the DA can prove in court. And you know damn well that your Peeping Tom video is not admissible. Anything you find from this video is the fruit of the poisonous tree."

"Sir." I rise from my chair and lean toward him over the desk. "These are evil fucking people. Someone has to stop them."

"That someone isn't going to be you." He lifts his right hand from the desk and extends it to me, palm up. "Badge and gun."

I hesitate for a moment, and he reiterates his demand with a more demanding tone, "Badge and gun. As of now, you're on disciplinary leave and are lucky that I'm not arresting you."

Tearing my badge from my belt, I angrily slap it into his waiting hand before pulling my gun from its holster. As I remove the clip, I let it fall to his desk and clear the barrel before slamming it on his desk.

"Stay away from them, Michales," he barks as I head to the door of his office, slamming it behind me.

Fat fucking chance.

CHAPTER TWENTY-SEVEN

GRANT

The gravel rocks crackle beneath my sneakers as I run the trail surrounding the estate.

I need to clear my fucking head.

My chest heaves as I push my pace.

She's a fucking toy. A disposable fucking toy.

Continuing to punish myself, billowing out my anger and exertion with every grueling step, as images of Will enjoying Abigail's body flash through my thoughts like a slideshow, shuffling with each tread of my feet.

His face between her thighs...

Hands gripping her hips...

The look on his face as he slid inside her.

Fuck!

Pushing myself even harder, I nearly sprint down the trail. Sweat beads at my temples and drips down my back, saturating my shirt. Reaching the clearing at full speed, I'm caught off guard when the phone in my arm band buzzes, cutting off the music playing in my headphones.

Slowing slightly, I continue toward the front of the estate and stand at the base of the steps for a moment to catch my breath.

Pulling out the phone, I swipe it to see an incoming text from Edmund.

> Where the fuck did you run off to last night?

As I'm weighing up my response, my phone buzzes again.

> I'm reaching out to that feisty little redhead from last night. She took my flogger like a fucking champ. Even with my cock in her ass and being suffocated from her face being buried in some little blonde bitch's ass.

> You would like her.

> You'll tire of her.

> Eventually we all do.

> And?

> When I do I'll get rid of her and replace her with someone else.

> What's going on with you?

> Liz made it sound like shit got weird but didn't elaborate.

Edmund might be my closest friend, but I am at a loss of how much or little to tell him about what transpired last night. And I definitely don't want it in a text where it can easily be shared with the others.

He's my closest friend. That doesn't mean he's a good one.

> You at the model today?

> Yeah, The Preserves. Trying to fuck this new agent I've got working for me.

> Thank fucking god you aren't Samuel.

> I prefer my women screaming voluntarily.

> I just went for a run, I'll meet you over there in about an hour.

Abigail takes the last of the steps into the foyer as I walk through the front door. Her hair is slightly disheveled. Her face dons no make-up. Her attire is a mere silk robe and a slim black leather collar wrapped around her neck.

She is fucking gorgeous.

> Maybe two hours

"Good morning, kitten." I step toward her and stop her at the bottom step, leaving us at nearly eye level. "Where are you headed?"

"To find you, sir." Her eyes are unwavering from mine.

"I went for a run." I pull the phone case from my bicep and drop it to the ground. "Did you need something?"

"No." She shakes her head.

"Did you *want* something?" I lift an eyebrow while slowly pulling on the silk sash that holds her robe shut. It falls open, the silk nestling against her breasts, leaving a gap between them. My eyes roam down the gaping fabric, from her pert cleavage to her now bare cunt.

Slipping my hands between the fabric, they slide around her hips, pushing the robe open and revealing her to me.

I fucking need her.

I can't even deny it from myself.

"Sit," I command while gently pressing on her shoulder to encourage her to do as I demand. She sits a few steps from the landing with her knees together, attempting to cover herself.

Kneeling down where I stand, I grip her knees and pull them apart, "You were made for my pleasure. Open your legs like a good little pet. Let me see and taste what's mine."

Gripping her thighs, I spread her wide with urgency, forcing her to fall back to her elbows. I delve my face into her sweet, pink cunt as my hands remain where they are, holding her open for me. The breathy moan that billows over her lips travels straight to my cock.

I need fucking more...

CHAPTER TWENTY-EIGHT

ABIGAIL

Grant pins my thighs open, the lip of the stair digging into my back as he feasts on me as though he is absolutely ravenous.

My fingers slide through his hair, damp with sweat, trying to push him away to decrease the pressure at which he is able to lick at my pussy. Snarling, he pulls against my grip and only sucks harder on my clit. Gripping his hair with both hands, I try to pull him from me as he forces me to come again.

Barely lifting his face from between my thighs, he growls, "Don't ever deny me what is mine, kitten. Or the next punishment might not be as enjoyable."

His words are immediately followed by a firm lick of my clit with the flat of his tongue. As he licks diligently at me, I gasp and my back arches off the steps as he presses his fingers inside of me. Drastically slowing the pace of his tongue, he works them both in tandem. Slowly teasing me toward another orgasm.

I hate how much I love his touch.

And how he knows exactly how to please and tease me.

"Scream for me kitten," his words purr over my clit as he vastly increases the speed at which his fingers drive and curl inside me. His tongue immediately follows suit, hurtling me toward yet another orgasm. Sliding my fingers back into his graying hair, I tug hard, trying to pull him closer as I grind my clit against his tongue.

He groans as I continue to pull him into me. Even if his groans are from pain, they don't cause him to relent in the least. If anything, he only swirls his tongue faster, demanding I give him what he wants.

There is no fighting it, screams of pleasure tremble over my lips just as he commanded.

"Such a good little pet," he lifts his face, covered in my arousal, and releases his firm grip on my thighs. Gripping my hips, he forces me onto my hands and knees. I struggle to keep my face from crashing into the steps beneath me as he tears the robe from me.

Clutching my throat, he pulls me upright onto my knees. I wince at the lack of cushion the hardwood beneath me provides. The silk of my robe passes over my face and Grant's voice is gruff when he commands, "Open wide for me."

As I open my mouth, the belt passes between my lips, and

Grant pulls it tight as he ties a knot at the nape of my neck.

"Hands," his voice is deep, sultry, and his commanding tone is almost hypnotic. I lift my hand, and he roughly pulls it behind my neck. The silk wraps around my wrist, securing it behind my head.

"I said hands." The bare skin of my ass stings as he slaps it. I raise my free hand and willingly place it at the nape of my neck. Grant wastes no time binding it with the other. The remaining tail of the robe falls down my back, followed by Grant's fingers trailing down my spine between them.

"This just won't do," Grant's arms slip around my waist, and he lifts me from the stairs. Carrying me a few feet, he sets me on the hardwood floor of the foyer and steps before me.

As he pulls the sweaty shirt from his body, he kicks his sneakers from his feet and pulls off his socks. With no fear of the hired help walking in on us, he shoves his shorts to the floor. I watch him stroke his already hardened length as he kicks them away.

Stepping to my face, he continues to fist himself while rubbing his tip against my lips. He grips my chin and presses himself into my mouth, as deep as the gag will allow. The saltiness from the residual sweat of his run assaults my tongue.

Yet, I wish I could take more of him into my mouth and please him the way he likes.

"Does my kitten need my cock?" he smirks as I struggle to wrap my lips around his shaft. Continuing to fight against the gag in my mouth, spittle rolls down my chin when he pulls himself from my mouth.

Walking behind me, he kneels between my feet. He rubs his wet tip against my entrance before pressing himself into me. My head is forcibly pulled back as he wraps the strands of the silk belt around his fist, pulling my head to his shoulder.

"I'm going to fuck you hard. Without mercy. Like I fucking own you," he gravelly whispers in my ear. "And you're going to take every last inch of my cock until I'm done with *my* cunt."

Using the grip on the bindings at the nape of my neck and a firm hand on my hip, Grant forces me to bend at the waist. His forearm rests on my back, keeping me bent over, he pulls on the silk—driving into me as he pulls me into him. He continues to yank me backward over his length, relentlessly driving into me. Every thrust deep and savage.

Painfully gratifying.

He might be fucking me for his pleasure, but that doesn't stop the orgasm he unleashes in me. Grunting and gnawing at the gag, I pull painfully hard against the bindings around my wrists. The release shoots through me so hard that my body trembles as he continues to unrelentingly thrust into me.

"Fuck, kitten." He continues his demanding strokes, grunting his words through his labored breaths. "You feel so fucking good when you come around my cock. So fucking good that I'm going to make you do it again as I fill you with my cream."

His hips pound against my ass, the repeated sound of our skin slapping together echoing through the hallway. The rapid slaps nearly drown out the feral noises spewing from us both. My screams are muffled by the wet fabric in my mouth as my pussy clenches around his length. Driving into me a final time, I feel his hips erratically twitch against me as he holds true to his word—filling me with his cum before withdrawing from me.

Standing behind me, he unbinds each of my wrists. My shoulders throb, pain radiating down my arms as I lower each to my sides.

"That sweet cunt between your thighs is fucking addicting, kitten." He places a heartless kiss against my temple and whispers into my ear, "Ensure you clean yourself up. I don't feel like fucking a cum-filled cunt when I return."

I breathe deeply as he walks away and close my eyes. Fighting back the tears I can feel welling behind my lids, I untie the knot behind my head and pull the wet gag from my mouth.

He told you himself, Abby...this isn't a fairytale.

He's not going to magically become Prince Charming and sweep you off your feet.

Grant is horrid.

A monster.

One of the cruelest men I've ever met. Yet his words and actions repeatedly slice through my heart. As hard as I try to fight it, I'm falling for him.

CHAPTER TWENTY-NINE

GRANT

Leaving Abigail in the hallway, I head upstairs to take a quick shower. Edmund will be expecting me shortly.

Reaching the landing, I pause.

An unfamiliar feeling washes over me—*guilt, maybe?*

But for what?

I've had more women than I can count, and not one of them has made me question myself like she does.

Not even Stephanie.

Waiting for the water to warm in the shower, I feel Abigail join me in the bathroom.

"What, kitten?" I question with my back to her as I check the temperature of the water.

"Can I join you, sir?" Her voice is soft and timid. "To make sure my cleanliness meets your approval?"

I gesture for her to enter the large walk-in shower, but I can't help but ponder her actual intentions.

I can't give her what she wants.

I've tried that once before.

It ended with a child I didn't want and a dead wife.

Stepping into the shower, I am overwhelmed with the intoxicating scent of her nectarine and honey-scented body wash.

A deliciously, sweet smell that lingers on her skin well after she bathes.

I find her under the warm spray of the water, suds rolling down her slick skin. If I hadn't just emptied myself into her a few minutes ago, the sight of her gliding the sponge over breasts would be enough to make want to slide inside her again.

"Give it to me." I grip her hand that's holding the soft, natural sponge. Without hesitation, she releases her grip and allows it to fall into my waiting palm.

After adding a generous amount of body wash to the already sudsy sponge, I turn Abigail away from me and swipe her wet hair over her shoulder. My hand traces down her spine, leaving bubbles in its wake. Repeating the motion, I draw almost invisible lines down her back. Once it is clean, I reach around her body and proceed to clean the front of her torso.

Kneeling behind her, I drag my hand up and down her legs before moving on to her perfectly round ass. Pressing between her slightly parted legs, I gingerly clean my cum from the uppermost part of her thighs. I place my hand into the stream of water to rinse it of the bubbles. I press two fingers into her and swirl them in a scooping motion to gather what I can of my release. When I pull them out, I rinse them in the water and clean her again with the sponge.

"All clean, kitten." I stand and thoroughly rinse the sponge. Hanging hers to dry, I grab the other for myself. "Go get dressed."

She turns to face me, and her emerald eyes pierce my dark soul when she looks up at me. Her voice is soft and timid as she places her hands on my chest. "Let me do the same for you."

I shouldn't...

Already fighting myself and knowing I need to distance myself from her, I hesitate to respond. Her gaze is unwavering as she stares up at me through her thick lashes, and I can't help myself.

Hesitantly, I lift her hand from my chest and provide her with the sponge. She takes it from me and places her hand back on my chest, using the leverage to trade places with me under the spray of the water.

Grabbing my soap, she squeezes a generous amount into the sponge. Kneading it to create foam, the woodsy scent mixes with her citrus and honey in the air.

The two of us smell delectable together.

Abigail drags the sponge from shoulder to shoulder, the suds falling over my pecs and down my abs. She follows them, tenderly cleaning the ripples of skin beneath her hand until she reaches my waist. Returning to my shoulder, she cleans down my arm to my fingers. Lifting my arm, she swipes along my armpit, and I can't help the smile that ticks at the corner of my mouth—her touch tickles.

Fuck, Grant...

Stepping closer, her tits press against my body as she snakes her arms around me. Wrapped in her embrace, she rubs the sponge over my back. Tipping my chin down, I'm met with those fucking green eyes again.

"Sir." She swallows hard. "I know what you've said—"

"Abigail." My tone is soft as I try to deter her coming words with my interruption.

"I know this isn't a fairy tale, and you're not a white knight." Her voice is pained as she continues to stare up at me. "I take you as the dark knight that you are."

"Dark knights have no qualms destroying everything in their path, kitten."

"I know..." Her voice trails off because she doesn't have to say the rest.

We both already know I've fucking broken her.

But it's what she's breaking in me that's fucking terrifying.

CHAPTER THIRTY

ABIGAIL

Grant's fingers grip my jaw and begin to lower his face to mine. His warm lips press against the damp skin of my forehead, and he places a soft kiss causing my heart to thump in my throat.

This isn't completely one-sided.

"I'll finish up, kitten." His lips vibrate against my skin as they linger on my forehead. Grant's hands slide down my arms as he softly pulls them from his body and takes the sponge from me. "Go get dressed."

Releasing my chin, he stands back from me, and I'm met with his blue eyes.

Cold. Icy. Blue eyes.

Doing as he asks, I leave him in the shower to finish up. I stay in the bathroom for a moment as I towel off and comb the knots from my wet hair before heading into the bedroom to gather my clothes for the day.

I pull open the top drawer of the dresser, and my fingers linger over the various shades of silk and lace as I select my panties for the day.

While Grant might not be all warm and fuzzy, he takes care of me. He doesn't keep me chained in the basement, living in my own filth as he uses me for his pleasure. Instead, he bathes me with expensive soaps, clothes me in luxurious garments, and keeps me in his bed. And while he does regularly use me for his pleasure, he fully enjoys the power he has over my pleasure as well. Nearly always forcing me to have multiple orgasms—apart from denial for punishments.

Grant walks into the bedroom as I'm lifting a pair of pale pink, silk panties adorned with black lace. His eyes appear to be approving as I slide them up my legs. Forgoing a bra, I walk into the closet to grab a maxi dress and a sweater.

"I like that one." Grant's eyes roll over the sleek, plum tank dress as I smooth it down my thighs, and I momentarily relish in his blessing. I pull the matching, cropped sweater on before returning to the bathroom to pull my hair into a messy bun.

By the time I return to the bedroom, Grant has dressed. He's wearing dark denim jeans, a well-fitted gray Henley, and a pair of camel-colored dress boots. Even when he's being casual, he always looks so put together.

"I need to go meet with Edmund for a bit." His fingers gingerly wrap around my throat. Squeezing gently, the damp leather of the collar rubs uncomfortably against my skin.

A humbling reminder of what it is that I am to him.

"Are you going to be a good little pet while I'm gone?" He uses his grip to tilt my face up to his.

"Of course, sir," I respond.

"Good girl," he grumbles before roughly kissing my lips. "I'll be back for dinner."

Grant walks from the room, and I question what to do now. He hasn't left me alone here in weeks, and this is the first time that he's ever left without putting me into the cage in the corner of the room.

Is this a test?

Do I put myself in there?

Or is he giving me free rein of the house without him being present?

Walking to the doorway, I stand at the threshold of the bedroom and the hallway, frozen with the decision that lies before me. My hands grip each side of the doorframe as I waver between my choices. Closing my eyes and taking a deep breath, I push myself into the hallway.

My fingers trail against the wainscoting as I casually make my way down the hallway to the next available door.

The room full of Grant's toys for me.

Stepping inside, it feels weird to be in here without Grant. Wandering around the room, there is so little that he has not yet introduced me to. Ropes, benches, nipple clamps, more vibrators and wands than I can count, anal plugs, that dreaded fucking Sybian machine he likes to make me ride…

What is that?

A red, leather box on a shelf at the rear of the room catches my attention. My fingers graze over the tufted lid, admiring the beautiful details of the engraved dark metal adorning the corners. Lifting the lid, it feels as though I am violating Grant's privacy. Yet, when I catch a glimpse of a photo of myself on the top, I can't stop myself.

Grabbing a handful of photos, the first few are of me. Each showcases the intricate shibari that Grant is such a fan of. Looking at the photos, I can see why—it's a beautiful art form. Continuing through the photos, each details his intricate knot work.

With so many different women.

The only relatable feature between them all is their eyes. They are all filled with so much terror, that I can practically feel their fear. All of them, except for one. Hers are filled with trepidatious adoration for the person behind the camera lens. I've seen that look before—in my own photos.

I've seen her before too. I just can't place where.

CHAPTER THIRTY-ONE

GRANT

Turning into The Preserves, I can't help but admire the development that Edmund is building on the outskirts of Adelaide Cove. While it's not quite isolated enough for my tastes, it is beautiful. Each plot is two or three acres, with a sprawling, brick, mini-estate.

This entire neighborhood is full of memories and dark secrets.

Making a left onto Topaz Circle, my eyes catch the third house on the left. A deep-red brick with well-placed ivy trailing down the corners.

314 Topaz. Final resting place of Madeline O'Rourk.

317 Topaz. Final resting places for Chloe Wilson and Cameryn Weathers.

Turn onto Opal Drive, my eyes are drawn to a taupe-colored brick accented with deep-red shutters and an impeccably well-manicured lawn.

597 Opal. Home of Paisley Allen.

Well, her final home.

There are perks to having a friend—with no moral compass—who has unfettered access to land, backhoes, and concrete. Buried deep in the foundations of these beautiful homes are the various women who have been unlucky enough to have crossed paths with Edmund, William, Samuel, Liz, or myself and became our playthings.

Some willing women who learned too much to allow them to return to their lives without putting the rest of us in danger.

The rest, unwilling women who met an untimely demise, sometimes as part of the games they were forced to play.

Plenty of room to continue to hide the casualties of our depravity.

Pulling up to the clubhouse at the rear of what has currently been built in this neighborhood, I park next to Edmund's car. There is another car in the lot, which I assume belongs to the agent he has working for him.

Stepping inside the clubhouse, there is no questioning the fact that he has gotten his wish about fucking her. He has her bent over the pool table in the middle of the room. Her shirt is lying on the floor, her black business skirt is hiked over her hips, and the remnants of her lacy panties are dangling from her hip. Handprints riddle her ass and thighs, which is currently the same shade of red as the estate at 314 Topaz Circle.

"Fuck. I'm going to cover this perfectly marked ass with my cum," he grunts while driving his cock deep inside her. He strikes her tender flesh again, and she lets out a pained yelp. Her eyes widen at the burning sting radiating across her ass. They widen further when she sees me approaching.

Gasping in horror at being caught in the act with her boss, she scrambles and tries to push herself up from the table. Edmund grips her hair and roughly shoves her face back into the felt of the table. She hits with such force it rattles the racked balls at the other end of the table.

"Don't you fucking dare," he snarls, "You're going to take my fucking cock until I'm finished. You're going to let him watch, like the dirty fucking whore you are, as I cover you with my cum. And if he wants to fuck that pretty mouth of yours, you'll take him down your throat like a good little cum slut."

"I'll pass." I take a seat in a large, upholstered chair. "But I'm more than open to seeing what a good little whore she is. Do you like being used? Or do you hate the enjoyment you get from being someone's whore?"

Her face grinds against the felt as he continues to pound into her and he growls, "Eyes on Grant. Give him the pleasure of watching your loathing, self-disgust for enjoying how I treat you."

His palm slams against her ass, only a silent scream escapes her mouth. Holding her head firmly to the table, he fucks her hard and forces her to come. Barely giving her the opportunity to enjoy it, he pulls from her and fists his cock until his cum splatters across her red and bruised cheeks.

Using his hand, he smears the cum over both cheeks like it's lotion before wiping his hand clean with the strands of her torn panties. He tucks himself back into his pants, releases his grip on her, and pulls her skirt back over her hips.

"The Carltons will be at 263 Ruby Court for their final walk-through in about ten minutes." He lifts her shirt from the floor and tucks it into the crossed arms attempting to cover her tits from me. "Clean yourself up and go take care of them."

"Of course." Her eyes dart to the floor, likely realizing how little that fuck meant to him.

"Sweetheart." A smirk spreads across his face as he calls after her, interrupting her already faltering gait. "If you want more of my cock or miss my sting on your ass, you know where to find me."

"You know I didn't come here to watch you dip your cock in your assistant, right?" I stand from the chair and walk toward Edmund.

"I've been trying to beat up that ass for weeks," he laughs. "I wasn't passing it up just because you had poor timing."

"You do plan to wash your hands before we go get lunch? Don't you?" I eye the hand he used to smear cum over his assistant's ass, and he merely smirks at me. I am slightly relieved when he leads me into the kitchen, where he promptly walks to the sink.

"Over lunch and a few drinks, I expect you to tell me what the fuck is going on with you," He thoroughly washes his hands while he talks. "First bailing out early last week, then declining what was going to be a rather enjoyable pre-lunch blow job."

He's right. I'm not myself.

CHAPTER THIRTY-TWO

ABIGAIL

Grant has been gone for hours. So long that the sun is beginning to set as I sit on the couch in the den and read a book about a hot, Scottish archaeologist.

Oh my God.

It couldn't be...

Sitting up, I slam the book shut and make my way upstairs. I walk down the hall, toward the room I shared with Garrison when I first arrived here—his room. Snatching the frame from the nightstand, I barely look at it before heading straight to the box of photographs in Grant's room of toys.

Opening the box, I rifle through the photos until I find the woman who shares the same adoring look as me. Lifting the frame and holding them side-by-side, there is no denying it. The bound woman is Garrison's mother.

Digging through the box, there are dozens of photos of her—the look on her face throughout them spreads the entire gambit of emotions.

But what order do they go in?

Were they a loving couple and she grew afraid of him?

Or was she terrified of him and grew to love him?

"Kitten?" Grant's voice carries through the house. I swallow the lump in my throat as I shove the photographs back into the box.

"Upstairs, sir," I call back to him as I put the frame in the box as well, not knowing where else to hide it right now.

His shoes thump against the steps, the thud of my heart matching his pace as he makes his way upstairs to me.

I position the box back on the shelf before grabbing a thick bundle of black jute from the wall. Trying to catch my unsteady breath, I toy with the end of the rope as Grant walks into the room.

"And what are you doing in here, kitten?" His voice is coy as he looks around the room before fixating on the heavy, bound rope in my hand.

"Nothing. Just looking around and passing time while I waited for you," I lie, immediately questioning why it pangs me with guilt.

"Bring that downstairs." He eyes the rope in my hands again. "I know just what to do with it after dinner. I had Victor turn on the heaters, so we can enjoy tonight's dinner under the stars by the pool."

He steps closer and lightly grips my jaw. Bending down, he presses his lips to mine, and I can taste his gin-scented breath on my tongue.

"Were you a good pet today?" he questions as he stares into my eyes.

Unable to gather a response, I nod.

Does looking through things and finding photos of your deceased wife bound and gagged count as being good?

I mean, he didn't say don't go through any of my things.

Jesus, Abby...

"Such a good girl." He smiles down at me with pride. Releasing my chin, he places his hand on the small of my back and leads me through the house and to the patio by the pool.

Stepping through the doors to the poolside patio, my skin immediately prickles with goosebumps from the cool, night air. A chill which is quickly removed as Grant pulls out my chair at the table, and I feel the warm air from the gas heater blow over me.

Grant takes his seat across from me, enjoying a slow, savory sip of his martini, and eats one of the mini pickled onions before questioning, "What did you do all day while I was out, kitten?"

"I read, mostly," I answer truthfully. "Did you have a good day?"

In an unusual response, Grant merely shrugs his shoulders. Before I have an opportunity to delve into it further, Victor walks onto the patio with our meal. He places the plates in front of us, eyes our drinks to see if we need a second, and promptly disappears.

Grant and I eat dinner in near silence. His eyes primarily trained on the plate before him or the bound jute at the edge of the table. While eating in silence isn't entirely unusual, I usually find his eyes on me or a hand on my thigh. Yet tonight, I get neither.

We've no more than finished dinner when Victor approaches to collect our plates. As he walks from the table, Grant tells him, "That will be all for tonight. Please ensure we are not disturbed."

Victor tips his head and retreats into the house. The moment he shuts the door, a chill runs down my spine as though the heater above me has been turned off.

"You asked earlier how my day was." Grant pauses to take a sip of his drink. "I watched my friend fuck some whore, went to a long lunch, and talked a great deal about you and the predicament that you have put me in."

"Oh?" I struggle to push out the word, my mind stuck on the possibility that he also shared in the woman.

While we aren't a couple, the idea of it tears me apart.

"What are you thinking right now?" He raises a brow, and it feels as though he already knows my thoughts.

"Did you—" I hesitate to ask, "Did you fuck her too?"

"No, kitten." His voice is sincere, with a tinge of annoyance. "That's the fucking predicament."

Not knowing what to say, my eyes dart between him and my drink as I play with the straw in my mule.

"I have told you several times that this" — his hand gestures between the two of us — "will never be some romantic love story."

"I know," I mumble the words.

"I've played house once before, in an attempt to appease a woman that wanted the great fairy tale." He rises from his seat and circles the table. Gripping my sweater, he pulls it over my head and helps me from my seat. Once I am standing, he gathers my dress to my hips and removes it as well. Leaving me standing before him in my panties and heels.

Grabbing the jute, he unbinds it and slips the end through the loop on my collar, pulling it through until he reaches the midpoint of the rope. "It ended with her dead. And me stuck with the child she was never supposed to have."

And just like that, I know the order of the photographs upstairs...

CHAPTER THIRTY-THREE

GRANT

Gathering both strands of the jute, I make a Cat's Paw Single Column of knots until I have a column to her navel. Releasing the jute, I gently spin her collar until the metal loop is at the nape of her neck. The column of knots falls down her spine.

My hands slide down each of her arms, pulling them behind her and crossing her wrists at the small of her back. Looping the rope around them into prusik cuffs, I secure them in place. Circling her, I gather the remaining rope around her waist, completely restricting her arm movement, and add a final clove hitch to secure it all. Bending down before her, I rid her of both her panties and her heels.

She looks so fucking perfect when she's bound for me.

"I have two choices with you." I usher her to the edge of the pool. She stares down at the deep water, her chest heaving and body trembling as I strip from my clothes.

Leading her to the steps at the edge of the pool, I take the first step into the warm water as her feet root in place.

"Sir?" Her voice trembles, and her eyes are filled with fear as I watch her swallow hard. "Grant?"

Gripping the column of knots running down her spine as a handle, I drag her into the water with me. She continues to call out my name and lightly thrashes her legs as I drag her deeper into the water. Not stopping until it is at my shoulders, I continue my thoughts, "Two choices, kitten."

Spinning her to face me, I spread her thighs and press my rigid cock to her entrance and shove into her to the hilt.

"I can dispose of you now." I pull the handle running down her spine until her face dips beneath the surface of the water. Her body thrashes—legs squeezing around my waist and her already tight cunt clenching around my cock like a vice. Lifting her face from the water, she gasps for air. "Or I can torture us both. Give in to your need for a happy ending until I'm bored out of my fucking mind and dispose of you then."

"Sir." The words bubble from her mouth as I push her back under the water.

I don't know the right answer, and it's not going to come to me with her writhing over my cock struggling to breathe.

I can't do that June & Ward Cleaver bullshit again.

Lifting her face from the water, I slowly thrust my cock into her. Struggling for clarity with the same ferocity that she is currently struggling to catch her breath.

"I don't want..." She gasps between heaving breaths, "As you are... Just yo—"

Her words cut off as I plunge her beneath the surface, forcing myself to make a decision. Even if it isn't the right one.

*Is there even a **right** one?*

Abigail doesn't panic. The only ripples across the surface dissipate when I stop thrusting into her. The water stills over her face, and I'm met with her emerald eyes. They are serene, not in the slightest distressed that this is how her life ends. Her chest constricts, as her body tries to force her to take a breath. A breath that will fill her lungs with water.

Still, no panic.

Meanwhile, my heart is fucking pounding in my chest.

She isn't like the others...

...She never was.

Pulling the rope, I raise her from the surface. She violently sucks in a deep breath of air as I grip her to my chest. Pushing the wet, matted hair from her face, she continues to draw deep breaths as I gravelly question, "What the fuck are you doing, kitten?"

She is too busy filling her lungs with air to answer me. Chlorine-scented breaths waft over my face, and I continue to hold her inches from my own, waiting for her response.

"Proving…to you…" She struggles to push out the raspy words, "I want…the…anti-tale…the villain."

For now…

Until you realize just how fucking deranged I really am.

"All of you." Her words become clearer as she catches her breath. "Every bit of darkness that flows through your veins as you take me willingly to hell."

With my fingers entangled in her wet, matted hair, I crash my lips against hers. They part readily, and I plunge my tongue into her mouth. Aggressively exploring every inch of her.

*Needing to reclaim her as **my** kitten.*

Using my tight fist in her hair as leverage, I violently yank her head back. My teeth scrape down her neck, and I pound up into her. Screams of pleasure billow from her lungs as I fuck her with a newfound vigor.

"Join me in hell, kitten." I nip at her neck before dragging her face under the water. Fast, hard strokes of my cock have her quickly clenching around me. Her release bubbles from her mouth, as she screams beneath the surface.

Her cunt quivers around my cock, and watching her fully give herself over to me, does me in. Roaring as I drive into her, my cock twitches as I fill her.

Roughly lifting her from the water, I continue to withhold her breath, as I kiss her hard and deep. I drag her lower lip between my teeth when I finally pull back, equally as breathless.

"You might be the perfect fucking pet, kitten." I breathe the words against her cheek.

CHAPTER THIRTY-FOUR

DETECTIVE MICHALES

Sitting at The Oak Tavern, I take a swig of my IPA as I continue to swipe through the dating app on my phone.

Regardless of what Chief says, there is no way in hell I'm not going to continue to work this case. They're all wrong. There is something going on with these people.

After being placed on indefinite leave, I decided to use some obscure methods to continue to work on this case without making any waves. I borrowed a few photos of a middle-aged model from his social media and created a dating profile for James. After spending a couple of days working my way through the well-known apps and finding nothing, it finally hit me.

My eyes scan over the photos of the three young women from the video that put me on leave. All of them are beautiful and young—college-aged young.

In what circles would they mingle with these wealthy, middle-aged men?

Ditching the well-advertised apps, I decided to move to a lesser-known, niche app. More correctly, an app to match sugar daddies with sugar babies. I've been waiting all day for them to verify my falsified credentials, proving I have the means to meet the qualifications they have for their Daddies.

Based on my assumed ages of them all, I extended my search area far enough to include the two universities that are within two hours of town.

I just need to find one of these young ladies.

Swiping through each profile, I pause to compare the faces against the photos I have sitting on the bar before me.

Just one to blow this whole fucking case wide open.

Finishing my beer, I use it to flag the bartender's attention. Kate pops the bottle cap off, eyes the photos before me questioningly, and sets the bottle down on the counter. Having watched me work many cases from the end of the bar, she doesn't say anything. She simply collects my empty and leaves me to my business.

Swipe.

Swipe.

Swipe.

Holy fucking shit.

I nearly swipe past the brunette without giving her a second glance, stilling my thumb seconds before she disappears with all the other women I've discarded in the past few days.

Lifting the photo from the bar, I hold one of the blondes next to my phone to compare the two. Taking my time and looking through the multiple photos she has on her profile, I compare them to the printed photo in my hand.

This has to be her.

Nikki, 21.

Graduate Student at UNC.

Clicking the button to match with her, I'm hoping the photographs I picked and my profile are good enough. I'm going on the logic that these women know about the wealth of Adelaide Cove, and my profile feels equally as douchey as those that I browsed for samples.

Guzzling a few gulps of my beer, I'm surprised – and excited – when my phone buzzes on the bar and displays a notification from the app. Swiping it open, I'm met with a photo of the blonde and a private message.

NIKKI

Hey baby

You're a rich tool that gets whatever you want, respond accordingly.

Pretty sure you're supposed to be the baby, beautiful

LOL

What do you want me to call you

Hopefully Daddy by the time you're screaming my name

For now, call me James

You think you could make me scream?

I'm fucking sure of it

I like a man with confidence in his abilities

Based on what I saw the other night, I'm sure she'd like just about anything if the right dollar amount was attached.

What is it that you're looking for James?

Someone to enjoy my weekends with, who won't be nagging me about the lack of time I have for them during the week.

What are you looking for, beautiful?

I feel like I'm soliciting a fucking prostitute on the street corner.

College is expensive, and rent is expensive in a college town. I can't always afford to spoil myself with shopping and vacations like I feel I deserve.

Smooth. Asking for tuition, rent money, gifts, and vacations.

Sometimes I like to enjoy my weekends or vacations with some friends. Are you open to socializing with my friends?

Depends on how good you treat me, but I'm always open to meeting new people.

Do they teach these girls a fucking class? How to Proposition a John Without Actually Asking for Anything 101.

So far you sound perfect, beautiful.

Dinner. Tomorrow.

Name the place. I'll come to you.

I'm tied up with class this week. Friday.

Nikolai's. 7 p.m.

Fuck, these men treat her well.

Make the reservation and I'll meet you
there.

See you Friday, beautiful

Is it really that fucking easy for these guys?

CHAPTER THIRTY-FIVE

ABIGAIL

"Are you ready, kitten?" Grant stands at the bottom of the stairs with a pre-dinner Gibson in his hand. "Our ride is almost here."

Of course I'm fucking ready!

This is the only the second time I'm leaving this house since I got here.

AND he's taking me to Greensboro for the night.

Stopping at the bottom step, his hand slides over the luxurious fabric of black Valentino dress covering my hip, before firmly gripping my ass. Not releasing his painful squeeze, he takes a sip of his drink before questioning, "Did you do as I instructed?"

"Yes, sir." I pause to take a relieving breath when he eases his hold. "The only thing I'm wearing are the items you left on the bed."

"Good girl." He smirks and places his drink on the table in the foyer. "I like knowing your sweet cunt is bare and ready for me."

A loud repetitive thrumping sound grows closer as Grant holds my coat out for me. Slipping my arms into the sleeves, I question, "What is that?"

"Our ride, kitten," Grant answers before leading me away from the front door. Passing through the house, he opens the door to the patio. At the far side of the pool sits a large helicopter with the blades slowing to a stop.

Ushering me through the door, he walks me to the helicopter with his hand on the small of my back. Climbing the steps, the inside is nothing like what I expected from the little I have seen of helicopters in movies and on TV.

Immediately to the left of the steps are two seats, one of which is occupied by who I am assuming is the pilot. To the right is a small cabin, similar in style to the plane I flew here on. It oozes luxury.

Something I am still not used to.

Grant is immediately behind me, leading me to a seat at the rear of the cabin. We've no more than sat when the I hear them seal the door.

"The flight will take about thirty minutes, sir," a man dressed like the pilot addresses Grant before taking a seat at the front.

A moment later, the blades begin to whirl and promptly

progress to the same thrumping sound I heard when it approached the house.

Thank goodness it's a bit more muffled.

Grant places his hand on my thigh and squeezes as we lift off. My eyes are glued out the window at the serene countryside as we fly over Adelaide Cove. Grant's hand slides up my thigh, and I gasp when his pinky brushes against the bare skin of my pussy.

"Shhhh," Grant's breath blows against my cheek as he leans closer, his finger continues to dust over my sensitive skin, "Part your thighs and let me play with what's mine."

My eyes dart to the two men, sitting no more than ten feet from us, and back to Grant.

"If you don't want them to know, you better be quiet. But if you don't part your fucking thighs like I nicely asked, they're going to be listening to you scream as you take my cock in your ass."

Spreading my knees, I part my thighs and take a slow, deep breath, waiting for him to press inside of me. Instead, he gently grips my wrist and drags my hand between my thighs. Gripping my chin, he whispers in my ear, "Play with your cunt. Show me how you made yourself come before you met me."

He places a wet kiss on my lips before taking the seat across from me, providing him with a better view.

I hesitate.

While I've fucked myself plenty before I met Grant, it's just always been with a vibrator of some kind.

I'm not a cavewoman.

Lifting my hand to my mouth, I suck on two of my fingers to coat them with my saliva before sliding them over my clit. My hips move knowingly in response to my fingers, and I quickly work myself to the edge.

Grant palms over the rapidly growing erection in his pants, obviously enjoying the show that I am providing for him. Continuing to rub over the bulge beneath his hand, he mouths the words, "Eyes on me."

Mewling whimpers tremble from my lips, and I am thankful for the sounds of the whirling blades above us for providing noise in this otherwise stiflingly quiet cabin. I hope they are drowning out the uncontrollable pleasure trembling over my lips.

Struggling to keep my eyes locked on Grant's deep blue pools for eyes, my thighs squeeze against my hand as pleasure shoots through me.

"Well done, kitten." Grant retakes his original seat and takes my hand. "Let me clean up your mess."

Sucking my fingers into his mouth, he licks and sucks every bit of my arousal from my hand.

"I hope you listened about drinking your water today too." His tone is serious. "Because I plan to use you as I see fit all evening. And then, maybe I'll fuck you too."

A devious smile spreads across his face.

It terrifies me, and I fucking love it.

CHAPTER THIRTY-SIX

GRANT

The helicopter touches down at Piedmont. While the co-pilot tends to the exit and stairs, I provide the pilot with our departure itinerary for tomorrow while Abigail exits onto helipad with a curious look on her face.

Waiting just beyond the helipad is a Bentley Mulsanne. As much as I despise having someone chauffeur me around, with the plans I have for tonight it seemed like the best option.

One I regret as much as I deem it necessary.

Sliding into the back of limousine after Abigail, the driver shuts the door behind us. We are barely alone when I press the button to close the partition.

"I'm still fucking hard from watching you play with that perfect cunt of yours." My hand rubs over my cock. I undo my zipper, pull it from my pants, and drag her toward me. "Come sit on my cock, like a good little pet."

Inching her dress up her thighs, she carefully straddles my lap and grips my shaft.

I'm not used to her hands on me and fuck does she ever feel good.

Using her grip to align it with her entrance, she slides herself slowly down my length with a needy moan.

A sentiment I wholeheartedly share.

She shifts her hips to slide over me again, and I roughly hold her still and snarl deeply, "I said sit, kitten."

Pulling her jacket from her shoulder, I bare her skin, leaving only a bit of it covered by the thin spaghetti strap of her dress. My lips and tongue dust over her naked skin, and needy whimpers tremble from her mouth.

My lips travel to her neck as I whisper in her ear, "Are you that fucking needy to come again so soon?"

"Yes," she groans. "Please."

"Then sit fucking still like I told you," I snarl. "Or you'll be begging me to let you come tonight. I'll keep you needy and wanting as I continue to fill you with my cream."

My lips and teeth continue to roam over her neck, shoulder and collarbone. Teasing her—taunting her to give in and ride me like she wants—but she sits unwaveringly still like the good little pet she is.

Little does she know how much I'm torturing myself too at this moment.

Sweeping her lightly curled hair out of the way, I expose the small lock at the nape of her neck, securing her collar. Dipping my hand into my jacket pocket, I retrieve the key and open the lock.

"Sir?" Her voice is soft but nervous as I remove the lock and pull it from her neck. Gripping the lapel of her jacket, I slide it back over her shoulder.

She's been collared for weeks, and she looks fucking bare without it.

"Time to get off my cock," I tenderly say as I place the collar on the seat beside me. Using my grip on her hips, I slide her up my shaft while fighting the urge to roughly drag her back over it.

Sitting beside me as I tuck my rigid cock back into my pants, Abigail's eyes fixate on the floor. She hangs her head as though she did something wrong and is awaiting the punishment that comes with my disappointment.

The car pulls to a stop, and a moment later, the driver opens the door. Stepping onto the sidewalk, I extend my hand to help Abigail from the car. Keeping her eyes on the ground, she takes her place beside me.

Gripping her chin, I tip her face up mine. Her eyes still face down as I ask, "Are you upset I took your collar, kitten?"

Without meeting my gaze, she nods in my grip. Gripping her face tighter, I forcibly kiss her lips. With them still nearly touching, I whisper against them, "Good."

A look of confusion spreads across her face as I release my grip and lead her into the building before us. The security door closes behind us, confining us in the small entryway. A moment later, the door before us opens, and Lorraine Hamilton greets me as we enter her shop, "Good evening, Mr. Geyer."

"Lorraine." I tip my head. She is a well-sought-after private jeweler. While her primary income stems from one-of-a-kind custom pieces, for the right price she also does private commissions.

"You must be Abigail." An envious smile spreads over Lorraine's face.

"Not to be abrupt, but we have a pretty tight schedule this evening."

"Oh. Of course, Mr. Geyer." She walks behind the counter and retrieves a black, velvet box. Setting it on the table, she slides it toward me. "I hope it meets your expectations."

"It isn't my expectations you need to meet." I slide the box to my left until it rests before Abigail. "It's hers."

Abigail eyes the box, her long slender fingers gliding over the soft fabric of the box. She flips the latch and holds the lid, hesitating to flip it open.

CHAPTER THIRTY-SEVEN

ABIGAIL

Unsure what it is that I'm going to find, I slowly lift the lid. Seeing the contents, I'm unable to control the gasp that expels from my lungs. My eyes immediately dart to Grant, and I swear, for a second, I catch a hint of a smile on his face.

Looking back to the box, I eye over its gorgeous contents. Lying before me is an intricate, platinum, chain-mail necklace with a diamond studded O-ring hanging from it like a charm.

A collar—made of platinum and diamonds.

It is heavier than expected when I lift it from the box.

"Allow me." Grant takes it from my hands and sweeps it around my neck.

"For the clasp"— Lorraine hands him a small black wand — "the magnetic frequency can only be opened with the wand. So, as I tell all of my customers who request it, I don't recommend misplacing it."

"She won't be taking it off. Will you, kitten?" Grant presses the clasp shut.

"No, sir." A smile spreads across my face as my fingers linger over the collar wrapped around my neck.

It silently speaks volumes regarding all the things that Grant will never say.

Even if that isn't his intention.

"It's perfect, Lorraine." Grant slips the wand into his pocket and shakes her hand. "Very discreet."

"It is one my favorite day collars that I've ever been commissioned to create. If you ever need anything else"— her eyes dart to my left hand—"you know exactly where to find me."

A ring?

No.

Surely, she was making some comment about 24-karat gold handcuffs or something.

"The remainder of your commission." She slides a slightly larger velvet box across the table to Grant.

Without opening the box, Grant looks at his watch, then promptly says his thank you's before ushering me to the car. Sliding into the backseat, he questions the driver, "Are we going to make it to our next destination on time?"

"I'll make sure of it, sir." He closes the door and quickly has us hurtling to our next destination. We ride in silence for several minutes, with Grant's hand resting securely on my thigh. Turning his upper body toward me, he slips his finger into the diamond circle dangling from my neck and roughly yanks my face toward his.

"I'm going to enjoy using this later." His lips pepper tantalizing kisses up my jaw toward my ear, and he whispers, "As you show me just how fucking thankful you are for my gift."

I gulp my next breath at the anticipation and trepidation of what he has in store for me.

When the limo pulls to a stop again, we are parked before a large historic theater. Once inside, Grant takes my coat and checks it. My hand wraps in the crook of his elbow and we walk through the massive, ornate lobby. I cannot shake the feeling that everyone is staring at the two of us —at me.

"Sir." I lean close. "Why are they staring?"

"I'm quite certain the men, and some of the women, are thinking about how much they'd like to fuck that tight little body of yours." He slides his hand to the small of my back as he bends his lips to my ear. "And some of them are eyeing the money draped around your neck."

I'm about to speak when the chandeliers above us repeatedly flash. Grant nudges me forward as he says, "Time to take our seats."

Most of the people in the lobby begin filtering into the sets of doors we continue to walk past, but Grant leads me to a set of stairs at the far end of the long hall. Only four other couples continue up them with us. An usher leads two of the couples to the first set of curtains, the other two leave us as we pass the next set. When we reach the final curtain, it is just the two of us.

The usher sweeps the curtain open. Stepping through, it is a private balcony overlooking the entire theater. There are four chairs, two along the rail and two offset behind them. As the usher allows our curtain to fall shut, I step toward the seats at the rail.

"Back here." Grant directs my attention to seats at the rear. Taking my seat, the lights in the theater go down completely, leaving Grant and I nearly obscured in the shadows of our private viewing area.

The lights of the stage come up, and the music of the orchestra beneath us begins to sound through the theater. All eyes are on the soprano belting out Italian on the stage, but Grant's eyes are solely on me.

"Come here." Grant's voice is deep and gravelly. Rising from my seat, I take a few steps and stand before him. His arm moves, and my eyes are drawn to his lap, where I find him slowly fisting himself.

"Sir?" My head spins, and my eyes quickly roam over the hundreds of people sitting beneath us and the half dozen in the opposing balconies.

Grant spins me where I stand. He pushes my dress up my hips, leaving me bare from the waist down. I am beyond grateful for the large chair before me I hope blocks the view.

"Get on my fucking cock, kitten." He drags me backward onto his lap as he slides himself inside me. His hands rub over my upper thighs, and he pulls them apart until I am reverse straddling him with my back resting against his chest.

He's quiet and still for a moment. His next words come as his slick fingers teasingly rub over my clit, "I suggest you are quiet and watch the opera, unless you want everyone to know what a needy whore you are."

CHAPTER THIRTY-EIGHT

GRANT

Her ass wiggles on my lap as I teasingly play with her clit through the recitative beginning movement of the opera. The music swells as the soprano on the stage begins her aria. Pulling my fingers from Abigail's cunt, I press them into her mouth. She eagerly sucks at them and coats them with her saliva.

Saliva that I return to her clit with firm, fervent, and fast strokes. Her hips twitch on my lap, only adding the friction of shallow thrusts of my cock into her.

Leaving me fighting my urge to fuck her over the railing before us.

Unable to control herself, a moan trembles over her lips.

"Is my kitten going to sing for everyone?" I increase the speed of my hand between her thighs.

"Sir..." she whimpers as her whole body becomes rigid, clenching around my cock, trying to hold back the screams she knows are coming. Screams I'm demanding from her.

Clamping my free hand over her mouth, I pinch her nose shut. Continuing to work my fingers, I thrust into her from beneath. Her warm breath blows hard against my palm, her cries of pleasure vibrating against my skin, as I force her to come. She sucks hard against my skin, trying to draw in more air as I still beneath her. Beginning to struggle, I force her to wait for the applause at the end of the aria.

Releasing her nose and mouth, her loud gasps for air are drowned out by the loud clapping from beneath us.

"I'm not done, kitten." She twitches at each soft, teasing swipe over her clit. "I am going to play with my pet as I please this evening."

Her chest heaves, and I watch her tits swell against the low-cut neckline of her dress. Slipping my hand beneath the fabric, I firmly pinch her taut nipple. Her head lolls on my shoulder, and I watch as she chews her lip.

"You're going to sit, quietly, with my cock buried inside of you."—I kiss the tender skin behind her ear—"as I play with your tender, swollen clit. Teasing you. Denying you and making you beg."

Needy moans grumble from her lungs as she already needs more from me.

"And if you're good for me until intermission and I don't hear a sound out of you, I'll take you in that private bathroom." I gesture to the door beside my chair. "And

I'll fuck your needy cunt until you're begging me to stop."

If I can make it to intermission...

Abigail's fingers claw at the arms of the tufted chair beneath us as I edge her for the eighth time. She's so fucking needy and sensitive that even with how timid my touches are, it takes her just minutes to be on the cusp of screaming for the audience beneath us.

A pleasure I would give them all if I didn't like this theater so much.

The final pre-intermission aria comes to an end, and I lift Abigail from my cock and usher her into the bathroom before the lights lift in the theater. Kicking the door shut with my foot, I unbuckle my pants and shove them down my thighs. I spin Abigail to face me and lift her legs around my waist as I drive her into the wall as I plunge my cock inside her.

She hits with enough force that it probably draws the attention of the attendees on the other side of it. I continue to drive into her hard and fast, both of us desperately needing to come after nearly an hour of edging. She eagerly takes each of my savage thrusts, her cries and my grunts filling the tiny space as we rattle the frames on the wall. Her nails claw at the shoulders of my suit jacket, my mouth swallowing each of her screams as every pent-up orgasm completely shatters her at once.

"One more, kitten." I increase the pace of my thrusts and fight the dire need to come inside her. She's so fucking sensitive it barely takes a minute before she's squeezing her thighs around my waist and clenching her tight cunt around my cock.

"Fuck," I snarl, tearing my cock out of her cunt before I spill inside it, leaving a mess for dinner. "Get on your knees and swallow my cock."

She eagerly slides down the wall and drops to her knees on the hard, marble floor. Gripping her wrists, I hold her arms above her head against the wall as she breathlessly takes my cock in her mouth and throat while I fuck her face.

"Every bit of you feels like fucking heaven when it's wrapped around my cock." I shallow my thrusts, keeping my cock in her mouth as I quickly creep closer to my release.

"Don't swallow," I grunt the words moments before releasing my load into her mouth with a breathy, "Fuck!"

Gripping her chin and using my hold on her wrists, I help lift her from the ground. Once she is standing before me, I tip her face up to mine and demand, "Open your mouth."

Her lips part and she opens her mouth, lightly darting out her tongue, proudly displaying her mouthful of my cum. I release my clutch on her chin and a slight smile tugs at the corner of my mouth.

"Such a good little pet," I smirk. "Go ahead. Swallow your cream, kitten."

CHAPTER THIRTY-NINE

ABIGAIL

Sitting in the back of the limo, my head rests on Grant's shoulder as his hand roams over my thigh. He has already exhausted me, in the best of ways, but I have no idea how I'm going to make it through the rest of the evening.

We still have dinner...

...and whatever else he has planned for this evening.

My eyelids are heavy, and I'm fighting the urge to take a tiny nap, which I am quickly denied when the car comes to a stop and the rear door is opened.

"Welcome to Nikolai's," a gentleman greets us as we step from the car. "Your name?"

"Geyer," Grant answers him.

"Please head inside." He gestures to the double wooden doors being opened behind him. "The hostess will take you to your seat."

Holy shit, this place is insanely fancy.

There is no line. No waiting for a table. The moment we walk through the doors, we are greeted with an immaculately put together woman who walks us straight to our table.

A booth...in the corner.

"I hope this table meets your request, Mr. Geyer." She fills our water glasses as Grant nods his approval. "Nikolai has requested to curate your menu for this evening."

"Please pass on my appreciation." She collects the two menus from the table as Grant speaks. She has barely stepped from our table when a waiter about my age approaches the table with a bottle of wine.

"2009 Chateau Le Pin Bordeaux." He presents the bottle to Grant. After giving his approval of the sample pour, the waiter pours a glass for us both before leaving.

"One glass." Grant's voice is firm as I take a sip from my glass. "I prefer fucking you when you're awake, but I'll have my way with you regardless."

I've woken with Grant deep inside me on several occasions, which is probably the only reason his statement doesn't carry any shock value.

Grant's hand drifts up my thigh, and my eyes quickly drop to my lap when he begins to move my dress as he moves. His pinky grazes against the tender flesh of my pussy and my thighs press together.

"Are you telling me no, kitten?" His voice is full of displeasure, "Because disobedient pets get punished, and Nikolai will have no issues with me tending to that punishment in the middle of his restaurant.

"No, sir. Never." I shake my head and part my thighs, granting him easier access to me than before. He doesn't hesitate to slip a finger inside me.

Toying with me yet again, he teasingly works his finger inside me as his thumb rubs over and around my clit. My fingers immediately grip the leather of the bench beneath me, each touch of my sensitive and already well-used pussy towing a thin line between pleasure and pain.

My chest heaves, and I chew at my lower lip, trying desperately not to make a sound in this crowded restaurant.

"Sir," I whisper in a panic when I see the waiter approaching our table. It doesn't deter him in the least. His finger twitches and rubs inside me as he discusses the appetizer being delivered as though he isn't currently two knuckles deep inside of me.

I think that's what he was doing. I barely comprehended a word.

Shit!

Did he just ask me a question?

My nails dig into the leather as I fight against the impending orgasm and force a smile, hoping Grant answers for me. The waiter turns to leave our table, and I breathe a slight sigh of relief that he won't be watching me come.

Clutching hold of Grant's wrist with both hands, I pull try to pull him deeper. He fights me long enough to slip another finger inside me. Holding him against me, he continues to curl his fingers as I ride his hand. I need again to come so badly that I don't care where we are.

What the fuck has he done to me?

"You're going to give me three for thinking you get to be in charge, or I'm pulling out of you right now," he growls in my ear. "Are you going to give me three?"

"Yes," I mumble the breathy word as I nod. He increases the friction of the fingers grinding over my G-spot and I come hard, squeezing violently hard around his hand as I fight to remain silent.

"Don't stop, kitten." Grant's voice is deep and demanding. "You owe me two more. Ride my fucking hand and take them like the greedy whore you are."

Fuck...

My thighs tremble, and his words shoot straight to my core, bringing me quickly over the edge.

"You get so fucking wet when I call you a whore," he gravelly whispers in my ear. "Do you want to be used like a whore?"

Yes...

"Getting fucked in all of your tight little holes at once?"

Yes...

But...

"Coming over and over," he whispers, and I can't deny how much the idea turns me on.

...even with how poorly it ended last time.

"A thick cock, filling that tight little cunt. And your mouth sucking another diligently as I stretch your ass with mine," he continues in my ear as I ride his hand so hard it's as though I'm trying to take his fist inside me. "Is that what you want, kitten?"

"Yes!" The word explodes from my mouth as I come again.

CHAPTER FORTY

DETECTIVE MICHALES

"Turn left in one-hundred feet." The computerized guide of the GPS speaks over the music playing through the speakers of the car.

I see the restaurant when I make the left-hand turn. Pulling into the valet at Nikolai's, I quickly realize that I am completely out of my element. My pickup truck stands out like a sore thumb between the luxury sports cars and sedans.

"Can I help you, sir?" the valet questions as I open my door.

"I have a reservation, Mic—" I cut myself off realizing I was about to provide the wrong name. "Carrington. Party of two."

He eyes my truck and my attire. While I pulled out and dusted off a suit for tonight, it looks like I pulled it off the rack from a discount box store in comparison to the other men walking inside.

"Listen, bud." I channel the pretentiousness I hate from each of the wealthy assholes in Adelaide Cove. "I got stuck in fucking traffic and my date is already inside. If you like your job even the slightest, you don't want me calling Nikolai to let him know how fucking incompetent you are."

"Please, sir. There is no need for that," He opens my door wider to allow me ample room to climb from the truck. "Please head inside and you will promptly be taken to your table."

"Mr. Carrington." A beautiful, well-dressed brunette approaches the moment I enter with a beaming smile. "Sorry to hear about the traffic, but glad you could make it. Let me take you to table."

Walking through the restaurant, I slow slightly as we approach a table for two with a petite blonde sitting with her back to me.

"Your table, Mr. Carrington." She smiles and continues past the table.

Taking my seat, the blonde across from me is undoubtedly the one from a few nights ago—the one I've watched countless times on the video for details.

She eyes me over with slight confusion, a polite smile spreads across her face before she speaks. "I think there might be a misunderstanding. I am meeting a Mr. James Carrington. They must have sat you at the wrong table."

"I'm at the right table, Nikki," I reply and watch her eyes widen.

She grabs her clutch from the table and is about to stand when I roughly grab her wrist and hold her to the table. Pulling my phone from my pocket with my free hand, I pull up the video of her foursome and press play.

"Unless you want this emailed to both your family and the entire UNC student body." I hold the phone in front of her face and provide her the opportunity to realize she's the one with a face in her cunt while she rotates her attention between sucking on Edmund's balls and licking the clit of the blonde riding his cock.

The moment she realizes she swipes for the for the phone and hisses, "Turn it off. Where the fuck did you get that?"

"I think you know exactly where I got it."

"What do you want?" The flirty coyness from our prior text exchanges is replaced with an eye roll and unpleasant annoyance. While that business conversation was light-hearted, this one is not.

"I think you know exactly what it is that I want." My voice is firm.

"Fine," she huffs and rolls her eyes again, before mumbling, "I knew that shit was too fucking good to be true."

Before I have a chance to question her statement, she continues, "I can't afford to pay you. I'll do almost anything to keep that video from ever being seen by anyone."

"Anything?"

"Yes. I'll fuck you to keep quiet." Her voice is quiet and raspy, "Once a week, max. You'll glove up because I am not getting knocked up by some middle-class fuck."

Not the anything I meant but based on the tent of my pants at the moment, my cock is quite intrigued.

"And your friends." I tap the screen on my phone.

This might be the easiest way to find the others and question them all.

"I don't know the blonde." She shakes her head. "I think her name was Riley."

"You had your face buried that deep in her cunt and you don't know her name?"

"Shhhh," she roughly hushes me and whispers, "No. I don't know her fucking name, okay. I wasn't there for her."

"The redhead?"

"Harper. She's my roommate." Guilt pains her face as she shares that information. "I'll text her, but she flew out to Vegas this afternoon. She's going to be...busy."

Swiping her little clutch from the table, I rifle through it until I find her license. I place it on the table and snap a photo of it with my phone.

"I know where to find both of you." I drop the ID back into her bag. "But I'm going to need some reassurances from you."

Finishing the last of the glass of wine sitting before her, she says, "Follow me."

With Nikki leading the way, we walk through the restaurant, pass through a set of double doors and a fire door until we're in a stairwell. She immediately drops to her knees, undoes my belt and begins undoing the zipper of my pants.

Fuck, Michales, this is a bad fucking idea.

Freeing my cock, she slides her mouth down it while the tip of her tongue drags teasingly along the underside of my shaft. She's relentless in her sucking, not stopping until she takes me down her throat and her lips kiss the skin at my base.

This sure as fuck doesn't feel like a bad idea.

Tugging at my balls as she continues to take me deep, I spill my release down her throat with a guttural groan.

"Is that enough reassurance for you?" She wipes her mouth with the back of her hand as she gets herself up from the floor.

The case, Michales...

"Thursday." I tuck my spent cock back into my pants. "Your apartment. Eight p.m.. I expect you and Harper to be there."

CHAPTER FORTY-ONE

GRANT

Pulling my fingers from Abigail's cunt, they are slick and glistening with her arousal. Holding them before her I raise an eyebrow and question, "Are you going to clean up your mess, kitten?"

She sucks every bit of herself from my fingers; her tongue licks between them and down my palm. She swirls her tongue as she takes them deep into her throat, and my cock twitches in my pants.

I've been fucking hard since she admitted to desiring to have all her holes filled with cock.

We have a party at the estate in a few days. I can make the arrangements with Liz. Abigail will get every bit of the fantasy she wants. It might just look a little different from how she pictures it.

"I'll give you a little break for the remainder of dinn—" I'm wiping the remainder of Abigail's arousal on my cloth napkin, when I'm momentarily distracted by a couple that passes our table.

He looks so familiar.

"Thank you, sir." Abigail takes a sip from her glass of water.

"Don't thank me yet, kitten." I take a bite of my prosciutto wrapped figs. She looks at me questioningly, waiting for me to divulge more as she takes a bite of the food before her.

"I was quite serious earlier." I pause as the waiters come to collect our empty plates and to replace them with our entrées.

"Shrimp and gruyère grits." The waiter places a plate before Abigail and then me. "With andouille sausage and truffle oil."

He leaves the table, and I continue as Abigail savors her first bite of the dish they left, "About letting you have all your holes fucked at once."

She abruptly swallows her food and stares at me for a moment with a slightly furrowed brow, her first words soft and timid. "But sir?"

"What's the matter, kitten?"

"The last time…," Her words trail off as she struggles to get them out. "When you shared me, you got so angry."

"You don't need to worry about that." I rub my thumb over her thigh as I squeeze it. "I ensure you it will not be an issue."

I know what the problem was.

I can remove it from the equation.

"There's a lot I can't give you give you, kitten... But delving into your depravity, tending to some of your sexual desires. That is something I can give you."

The man who caught my eye passing our table now storms through the double doors by our table.

Detective David Fucking Michales.

Quickly pulling my phone from the breast pocket of my jacket, I click open the camera app and start recording. Holding it as though I'm taking a photo of Abigail, I wait for the woman to follow behind him.

I don't have to wait long. A young, petite blonde walks through the door. She's beautiful, elegant, and confident.

Exactly the type of woman Liz would procure for us.

"I need a moment, kitten."

Hastily, I crop down the video and send a text to the group chat.

> We have a problem

EDMUND
> I told you how to take care of that

> Not THAT

> I just saw Michales at Nikolai's

SAMUEL
> So? What's the big deal?

LIZ

Detective Asshole can't afford a fucking glass of water there, you idiot

> He was with this woman
>
> Do we know who she is?

I send the video to all of them.

EDMUND

Don't think so

LIZ

Jesus Eddie, you fucked her.

Maybe next time grab a picture of her cunt so he can remember

Her name is Nikki. I'll call her in the morning and we can all meet for dinner at the estate.

> Seven

LIZ

Business only.

EDMUND

That means your cock stays in your pants kid.

Before I put my phone away, I send another quick text just to Liz. I want to provide her enough time to procure exactly what is needed for my kitten.

LIZ

Interesting.

You've piqued my interest Mr. Geyer.

Watching or taking?

Use your imagination sweet child

I intend to

CHAPTER FORTY-TWO

ABIGAIL

Finishing dinner, Grant passes his black card to the waiter without looking at the bill. He quickly returns with the receipt for Grant to sign, and I audibly gasp when I glance at the total.

$7523.34

"It was a six-thousand-dollar bottle of wine, kitten." He signs the paper slip without hesitation. "And the gratuity and sommelier fees are included."

"I didn't even finish my glass." I reach for it, but Grant lightly grabs at my wrist.

"And you aren't going to." He pulls me from the booth. "Dinner is over, which means so is your break."

With his hand possessively resting on the small of my back, he leads me through the restaurant and obtains my jacket from the coat check. Slipping it up my arms and over my shoulders, he places a soft kiss against the side of my neck. "I'm look forward to finally getting you out of this dress."

Stepping from the restaurant, I'm surprised that the limousine isn't waiting for us.

"Nikolai has some private suites next door. They are nicer than any hotel in town, and where I prefer to stay when I come here."

Grant surprises me in the elevator. Even though empty, his hand simply remains comfortingly on the small of my back. The doors open, letting us directly into the main area of the suite.

It's fucking beautiful.

As I take in the white marble floors, floral arrangements, and art decorating the walls, Grant slides my coat from my shoulders and places it folded over the arm of a nearby chair.

"Oh my god! That has to be the most impressive reprint I have ever seen." I cross the room to get a closer look, nearly squealing when I stand inches from it. "Is this? Is this a fucking Pollock?"

"I don't know if I've ever seen you this excited about anything." Grant stands behind me and peppers kisses down my neck while I fight the urge to touch the work of art before me.

"Grant. Sir," I correct myself. "This is Number 17. The closest I've ever come to seeing a Pollock was from about ten feet away at the Museum of Modern Art."

Pulling the zipper at the back of my dress, he slips the straps from my shoulders and lets it fall from my body. Leaving me in nothing but my heels as I stare at the painting before me. His hands roam over my body while I continue to stare at the Pollock in awe.

A nip at my shoulder draws my attention back to Grant and the warm, wet kisses he's leaving on my neck. His teeth graze my ear lobe, and he whispers, "Do you intend to stare at this painting all night? Or are you going to join me in the other room where I intend to make you a work of art?"

Taking my hand, he leads me from the painting. My heels click on the marble floor as I follow him into the bedroom. Laid at the edge of the ornate, Medieval style bed are numerous strands of black jute.

Undoing the first strand, he makes quick work of tying an intricate chest harness. He kneels before me and ties another bundle of jute around my waist and thighs. Climbing onto the bed, he tosses two of the remaining ropes over the rails of the canopy above and connect them with large metal clips.

Grant holds out his hand for me. When I slip my hand into his, he pulls me onto the bed and promptly secures one of the metal clips to a loop on the ropes running over my chest. He clips another to a loop below my stomach. A quick tug of the rope, another metal clip and Grant has me suspended above the bed. Grabbing the last section of rope, he binds my ankles and wrists to the ropes running around my thighs. When he's done, I hang helpless, all of me on display for him to admire and use as he pleases.

Just as he said.

He gives me a gentle tap, leaving me swaying in the ropes as he climbs from the bed. Viewing me from all angles, he smiles with contentment and removes his clothes.

"Fucking perfection." He stoops below my line of vision, and I hear him rustling through the leather bag that would be at his feet. When he returns to me on the bed, he is holding a stainless plug and a small bottle of lube.

Stepping between my parted thighs, he squeezes lube over the plug and teasingly works it inside my ass. Once situated, he toys with it a little as his tongue flicks at my fully exposed clit. His mouth between my thighs hard, soft, teasing, and brutal—as he repeatedly changes the pace of his licking and sucking with each orgasm he forces from me. Writhing and tugging at the ropes binding me, I scream as he painfully makes me come again.

"Are you ready for my cock, kitten?" Grant stands and aligns himself with my entrance. His tip presses against me as my thighs continue to tremble uncontrollably. Without waiting for an answer, he slams into me.

So fucking full with both him and the plug filling me.

Using the ropes wrapped around my hips and the suspension to his advantage, he fucks me hard. Each thrust more savage than the last. My whole body shakes in the swing made of ropes, tears of pleasure rolling down my face as another wave of euphoria begins to creep within my reach.

"That's it." His grunted words rattle between his thrusts as my orgasm tears through me, "Squeeze that tight, little cunt around my cock so I can paint my masterpiece."

Pulling me tight, he buries himself to the hilt as he fills me with his cum.

Still catching my breath, he lowers me to the bed and makes swift work of removing all of the ropes from me. Lying against me, his lips pressed against my temple, his fingers trace the temporary divots in my flesh from the ropes.

I struggle against the heaviness of my eyelids, but Grant has fucked me well beyond exhaustion today. His deep voice vibrates against my skin, but I'm unable to comprehend his words.

"What?" The mumbled word passes my lips as I drift off to sleep.

CHAPTER FORTY-THREE

GRANT

Holding Abigail against me, my fingers linger over the marks she entrusted me to leave on her skin. Placing soft kisses along the side of her face, down her neck and shoulder, the words spill from my mouth. "Taking you was the best decision I've ever made."

A heavy moment of silence is followed by Abigail dreamily mumbling, "What?"

Lifting my head from the pillow, I find her eyes closed and realize that she has already fallen asleep.

It's probably best you didn't hear me.

I pull the blanket at the foot of the bed over the two of us and she rolls against me, nuzzling her face into the warmth of my chest. Instinctually, I wrap my arms around her and pull her closer.

What the fuck has she done to me?

Holding her close, I fall asleep faster than I have in years.

———

Abigail's bare ass rubbing against my cock stirs me from my sleep. As if I didn't just fuck her hours ago, my cock is firm and rigid against her. Soft moans come from her as she continues to grind against me.

"Are you having sweet dreams, kitten?"

"Mmm." Her back arches as she continues to grind against me.

"Dreaming about my cock," I whisper more to myself as I press the head inside her, stilling when she winces lightly in her sleep.

"Is that sweet little cunt of yours too sore from last night?" I slowly twirl the plug still stretching her ass and I'm delighted when her needy moans return.

Grabbing last night's lube from the bedside table, I pull the blanket from me and thoroughly slather it over my tip and shaft. Gently, I play with the flared base of the plug, teasingly thrusting it to stretch her tight hole. Her moans and whimpers only urge me to bury myself inside of her.

"Are you dreaming about my cock fucking your ass?" I whisper as I continue to fuck her with the toy.

"Mmmhmmm." Her response is dreamy.

Slowly pulling the plug from her, I immediately replace it with the head of my cock before pulling the blanket back over me. Still enjoying her dream, she pushes her ass against me and takes me deeper into her ass. Holding her hip, I push against her until she's taking every inch of me.

"Ssssssh. Go back to sleep, kitten, and let me fuck this tight little hole in your dream."

Soft groans continue to vibrate in her chest as I leisurely take her ass. Each time I still my thrusts, she rocks her hips to continue taking my cock.

Continuing to take her ass with slow, tender thrusts, she begins to stir.

I want more.

I fucking need more.

"Time to wake up, kitten." I kiss along her shoulder. "I want to thoroughly fuck this tight little ass of yours, and I don't want you to miss it."

Increasing my tempo slightly, her eyelids flutter. Stroking the hair from her face, I kiss her cheekbone and question, "Do you like waking up to my cock in your ass?"

"Yes." Her response is sluggish as an embarrassed smile spreads across her face.

Gripping her hip, I firmly slide the entirety of my length into her, and she groans my name.

Fuck that's an amazing sound.

"I love fucking this tight little ass." I drive into her again. "Knowing that no one else will ever know how fucking sensational it is."

Pleasing groans and whimpers blow from her with each continued thrust. Pushing her onto her stomach, I roll over her back and work my way to a punishing pace.

Burying her face in the mattress to muffle her screams, her fingers claw at the sheets as she squeezes around me.

"Are you becoming my little anal whore, kitten?" I continue my fast, deep thrusts into her ass as she continues to push back into me.

"Yes, sir." She bucks her hips against me.

"Fuck!" I drive myself in to the hilt, filling her ass with cum.

Carefully pulling out, my release trickles from her hole and drips over her visibly swollen cunt. Kissing down her spine, I roll from her before pulling her back into my embrace.

"You should probably go shower and clean up." I loosen my hold on her. "It's getting late, and the car is going to be here in about an hour to take us back to the airport. And there's going to be quite a few things that I need to tend to when we get home.

Abigail rolls from my embrace and grimaces as she climbs from the bed, her soreness extending well beyond her cunt and asshole.

She took more than I thought she would.

Than I ever dreamed she could.

CHAPTER FORTY-FOUR

DETECTIVE MICHALES

Tacking the photo to the wall, I take a step back and scan over all of them.

My suspects...

Grant Geyer

Elizabeth Beaufort

William Cattaneo

Samuel Millington

Edmund Parker

...and the three women that are going to blow this case wide open.

Nikki Sloane

Harper Jenkins

Riley???

Having learned that both Nikki and Harper were UNC students, I painstaking went through years of student body photographs. But I did not find a single student that even remotely resembled the third blonde from the video.

A quick call to Nikki's landlord this morning, under the guise that I still had full authority of my badge, didn't lead me much further than acquiring Harper's last name. The lease is only a few months old, they have no additional co-signers, and received prompt approval because they paid a year of rent in advance.

Where did they get that kind of money?

My phone buzzes, and I'm excited to see Nikki's photo from the sugar baby app sitting on my screen as a notification.

More excited than I should be.

Swiping it open I'm met with a single message.

NIKKI
I talked to Harper

Dots appear and disappear, indicating that she repeatedly pauses as she types her message.

What did she say?

She wants to see the video

Give me your cell phone number

919-364-3946

Copying the number, I close the app and send her the video via text.

Pressing play once it sends, I watch the video while I wait for a response. I'm just passing the moment where Harper, who is getting thoroughly fucked by Edmund Parker, lifts her face from Nikki's pussy when a text pops up on my phone.

> She said she'll do whatever you want.

> I'm going to need to hear it from her

A FaceTime message begins to ring on my phone. Accepting the call, I'm met with a very upset Harper. She looks as though she is going to cry and scream.

"Like Nikki said, that video can't get out. I'll give you everything she offered."

"What kind of confirmation are you going to give on that?" I question.

"Well, I can't exactly suck you off over the phone now, can I?" she snarks, divulging just how much of last night Nikki shared with her.

I've been pushing thoughts of Nikki's mouth wrapped around my cock away since I woke up this morning.

Letting it happen was a horrible fucking idea.

Shitty police ethics.

But technically, I'm not a fucking cop anymore.

"I'm going to need something," I rebut, "I need you to take a little initiative like your friend, Nikki, and tell me a bit about what is happening in this video."

"I'm getting fucking railed while eating out my roommate." She exhales loudly as she closes her eyes. "Is that what you want to hear?"

"I'm going to need more, Harper." I leave the statement open for interpretation.

I want to know why? Who's the other blonde? If you don't know her, how'd you all wind up together?

But my cock is at full attention, and I'll happily take something I shouldn't over a dive through online porn.

"Nikki," she calls for her roommate. "He wants more."

"Prop the phone on the table," Nikki instructs as she slips from her tank top. "I'll help you give him what he wants."

Fisting my cock, I watch the two of them pleasure each other as my eyes occasionally roam over the photos posted on my wall.

I'm getting so fucking close.

CHAPTER FORTY-FIVE

GRANT

Pulling up to the estate, the only other car parked in front of the house belongs to Edmund. He must have just arrived because he's stepping out as I pull to a stop.

"My cock is like one of Pavlov's fucking dogs," Edmund blurts out the words the moment I open my door. "He gets all excited as soon as I see this place."

"It's a business night. Keep your cock in your pants," I huff. "And fucking far away from me."

He laughs as we make our way to the front door. As usual, cocktails are waiting for us when we walk through the door. Each of us collecting ours, we make our way to the dining room—which is our makeshift boardroom of sorts.

"Did you take care of *your* problem?" Edmund questions as we take our seats. "I'm assuming no, since you never called to know what foundation to put her in."

"Almost."

"Almost?" Edmund repeats my response to me. "Are you going soft in your old age?"

"I hear they make a pill for that," Liz quips from the doorway.

"My cock is anything but soft, sweet child," I snark at her, as she and Will take their seats.

"Where's the kid?" Edmund questions.

"Right fucking here." His words are slightly slurred.

This kid is going to be a fucking problem.

I still can't fathom why Liz lobbied for him to join us.

"Nikki should be arriving in a few minutes." Liz speaks over everyone. "Are we all up to speed so far?"

Unanimous yesses echo around the round as we all respond to her. The doorbell rings and a moment later the butler escorts her into the room. It's the redhead entering behind her who immediately draws Edmund's attention.

"You were supposed to come alone." Liz's tone is abrasive.

"I'm sorry," Nikki mutters. "I didn't know how to get back in touch with you. You're going to want to talk to Harper, too, after this morning."

"What were you doing with the man at Nikolai's?" I question.

"I met him through an app that matches men like you to girls like us." She begins her story. "Only the man that arrived was not the one I was talking to. I was about to bail when he showed me a video."

"A video?" Liz questions.

Nikki pulls out her phone, pulls up the video and slides her phone across the table. On it plays a shaky video of her, Harper, Edmund, and another blonde all thoroughly enjoying one another.

That fucker.

Edmund passes the phone back to her and she continues, "He threatened to share it with my family and all of UNC if I didn't give him what he wanted."

"And what was that?" I ask.

"Sex to keep quiet."

"And you agreed?" Liz lifts a brow.

"Yes. To a weekly fuck. But then he wanted to know who the other girls were. I was so in shock over the video that I blurted out that Harper was my roommate, and I told him I didn't know the other girl. I didn't say anything about any of you. Nothing. I swear."

"While you aren't supposed to discuss the other women you meet here, they weren't covered under the NDA you signed," Edmund answers the question she hasn't outright asked.

"Thank God," she sighs, learning she isn't currently on the hook to repay us a million dollars.

"The backroom?" I question.

"He wanted proof that I was going to hold up my end of the agreement, so I blew him in the stairwell."

"Probably the best fucking head of his life," Edmund whispers to me and I silently shake my head.

"And Harper?" Liz asks.

"I messaged him this morning to let him know Harper was on board because he told me he was willing to expose her too," Nikki answers for her. "He watched us finger each other to prove her agreement, and he's expecting both of us to pay up on Thursday when he comes to our apartment."

"And you're going to give whatever he wants." Liz smiles at the two of them.

"You aren't going to do anything?" Harper finally speaks up.

Liz crosses the room and firmly grips Harper's face, her long nails dimpling the skin. "You get to keep your million dollars. Is that not enough for you, princess? Considering you fuck drunk frat boys for flat beer, I'm thinking two grand a week is more than sufficient."

Liz eyes the table for agreement, and none of us disagree.

"You don't speak a fucking word about the five of us or what happens in this house. You'll zealously take his cock in all your holes. You'll fucking suck his toes while Nikki eats his ass if that's what he wants. Understood?"

"Yes, ma'am," Harper painfully responds, and Liz places a firm kiss on her lips before releasing her face.

"We'll be in touch, ladies." Edmund nods his head toward the door, instructing them to leave. Meanwhile, I can't help but wonder if he's still going to give the redhead a call knowing she's fucking Michales.

It's a fucking power play. Of course he is.

CHAPTER FORTY-SIX

GRANT

"We should just fucking kill him," Samuel says his first words since sitting at the table.

"He's a fucking cop," Will smacks him on the back of the head. "You can't just kill cops in a small fucking town like this and not expect to get caught."

"They'll give him what he wants." Liz's voice is pragmatic. "It'll keep him content and quiet for a bit while we figure out how to handle him."

"I hate to agree with the stupid kid on this one"—Edmund interjects—"but eliminating the problem really might be the easiest solution. Not immediately, but after enough time that we could pin it on the girls for the blackmail."

Not a great idea.

But not a terrible one.

"If we go that route, the video gets leaked, Eddie." Liz tries to negate his idea.

"Did we watch the same video?" Edmund smirks. "An hour-long video of my thoroughly fucking and pleasuring three different women: that's like a fucking dating ad for more pussy than I can fucking handle."

"I have the connections." Will changes the subject. "I'll reach out to some guys I know about security. The fuck being able to stand outside the window and record what he saw is the first issue."

"The first issue is how he knew we were here in the first place." My eyes dart to Samuel, who continues to draw the attention of the Adelaide Cove Police Department.

He's the fucking problem we need to deal with.

"Don't fucking look at me like that, old man," Samuel snarls.

"Do you need a fucking reminder?" I plant my palms on the table and rise from my seat, ready to climb across this table to drive my fist into smug face.

"Boys," Liz yells over both of us. "Measure your cocks somewhere else. He's right though, Samuel. You don't need to keep your cock in your pants, but you need to sure as fuck ensure the women you're putting your cock in are willing participants outside of this house.

"Fucking make me." He storms out of the room, leaving the four of us seething at the table.

"How the fuck did he pass vetting, Liz?" I gesture toward the door. "He has zero fucking self-control."

"He's fine," she attempts to calm me. "I'll take care of him. I'll get him in line."

"You're not going to fuck him into obedience." Edmund stares at her as he speaks. "That well-worn cunt between your thighs isn't fucking magical."

"Fuck, Eddie." A flirtatious smile spreads across her face. "You know what to say to melt my panties. Keep it up and I might not even need a little sword crossing between you and Will to finally let you see how fucking magical it is—"

Will's eyes angrily dart to Liz, and she immediately ceases her flirting with Edmund.

"Besides." She smirks at me. "Based on Mr. Geyer's requests for this weekend, I'm quite certain I'm going to have the option of watching one of you gentlemen get thoroughly fucked in the ass. It just happens to be the last of you I expected."

"I have no intention of getting fucked in the ass this weekend," I correct her and watch disappointment spread over her face.

"The lot of you are so fucking boring sometimes." Liz rolls her eyes. "Please don't tell me all of that is for that little blonde thing you had here last time."

"Then don't ask," I gruffly respond.

"You're ignoring all of my advice then," Edmund questions.

"She's different." I shake my head, both in disbelief that I'm saying the words and that I actually believe them. "She's one of us."

"The fuck she is." Liz rolls her eyes again. "She's a fucking angel compared to all of us."

"Lucifer was an angel once, too."

Liz isn't entirely wrong.

Abigail is sweet.

Kind. Smart. Funny. Talented. Agreeable.

There is a pureness about her that I have never once found a glimmer of in myself.

But there is a tinge of darkness pumping through her veins. I see it every time she leans further into my depravity, even if she doesn't yet know it's there.

She is drawn to my darkness, enjoying every devious and depraved act I push upon her—and they slowly feed the darkness growing inside of her.

CHAPTER FORTY-SEVEN

ABIGAIL

I can't get enough of the conservatory at night. This far outside of town there is no light pollution, and I can see every star in the sky above me. I couldn't ask for a better place to paint.

Stacks of canvases are accumulating against the walls. My need to create only growing with each passing day. Looking over the paintings, I realize how much my work has changed since I met Grant—since Grant took me to be his pet.

They are darker.

Each displaying different variations of Shibari knots and bondage. Couples entwined in the throes of passion. Orgasms. Contemporary representations of the sexual lifestyle that Grant has introduced me to.

But they are rich. *Deep*.

And the absolute best things I have ever created.

Sweeping my brush, I glide the oil paint down the massive canvas on the easel in front of me. I'm still prepping it, spreading black paint across the entirety of it as I mentally plan the image I plan to add to it tomorrow.

"I fucking love watching you paint, kitten." Grant's voice startles me from the doorway.

"Is it my artistic genius?" He eyes me suspiciously as I continue to work my brush over the canvas, "Or the fact that I prefer to do it in the nude?"

From the corner of my eye, I watch him meticulously roll up the sleeves of his shirt, exposing his forearms. Stepping behind me, his hands roam over my naked body as I attempt to continue working.

His fingers dip between my thighs as he reaches for the brush in my hand, "I think you're done for tonight. I want to play with my pet."

"Five more minutes." I pull the brush from his reach. "I'm almost done."

"Now." His voice booms, rattling the conservatory glass as he tears the brush from my hand and throws it on the table. Grabbing the almost black canvas from the easel he tosses it to the floor. "You know how I feel about disobedient pets."

"I'm sorry, sir." My eyes fall to the floor.

"You will be." He forces three fingers inside of me, painfully stretching me as he relentlessly finger fucks me. My legs tremble as he forces a never-ending string of orgasms from me.

"Sir," I plead as I nearly go limp against the arm wrapped around my waist. "I'm sorry."

Ignoring my screams and blubbering apologies, he doesn't yield. It only fuels him, evident by his hard length rubbing over my ass as I convulse uncontrollably against his arm.

Finally pulling his hand from between my thighs, he continues to hold me flush to his body. Swiping his hand over my face and breast, he smears my arousal across my skin.

"You still want to fucking paint?" He grabs a large tube of white paint and single-handedly unscrews the cap, letting it fall to the floor. Squeezing the tube aggressively in his hand, he expels the full contents on my chest. He drops the tube at my feet and roughly spreads the oil paint over my skin. His hands smear it over my breasts and down my stomach, not stopping until his large palm covers my face.

Releasing his hold on me, my legs still shaky, I fall to the floor.

"Crawl to your fucking canvas." He looms over me. Paint smears across the front of his pants as he undoes his zipper and pulls out his hard length. "Get on your fucking stomach. Ass up. Let's fucking paint."

Lying in the middle of the canvas, Grant uses his knees to push my legs apart and my skin slides through the slick paint over the rough canvas. Settling between my thighs, Grant shoves himself inside me.

Gripping my wrist, he swipes my hand over my face and slaps it against the canvas above my head. His fingers tangle into my hair, and he forcefully holds my face against the canvas as slams into me. Each thrust smears the white paint on my body into the blackness beneath me.

Spreading his body over mine and pinning me to the canvas, Grant continues to drive into me. I continue to cover paint across the canvas as my body writhes beneath him with every orgasm he forces from me.

"Fuck," he roars, driving into me with such force that my eyes water, as he empties himself inside of me.

He kisses over my shoulder and up my neck as he lifts me from the canvas. Holding my back to his chest, he continues to kiss my neck until he reaches my ear.

"This might be favorite one yet," he says softly into my ear before spinning me to face him.

Brushing the matted hair from my face, he pulls me tight and I mutter, "Your suit."

"I think it's a little late for that, kitten." He releases his tight hold. Stepping back, I find that he is covered in nearly as much paint as me.

"That's why I paint naked." I shrug with a smirk, before heading upstairs to the shower.

CHAPTER FORTY-EIGHT

DETECTIVE MICHALES

Following my GPS, I make my way to Nikki and Harper's apartment. Seeing that it's only a few buildings up the block, I pull into the parking garage on my right. I climb from the truck and walk the half block to their building.

Stepping inside as the doorman pushes open the door, I immediately realize that I am out of my element again. There are two elevators at the rear of the lobby, both of which require passing the security desk first.

These guys look more like ex-special forces than frumpy retired cops.

"Can I help you, sir?" the guard behind the desk calls to me.

"Yes." I cross the distance and lean on the counter above his desk, "I'm here for Apartment 3B, Nikki and Harper."

"Are they expecting you?"

"Yes."

Lifting the phone, he calls their unit. He gestures to the elevators after hanging up. "Third floor. It's the apartment on the left."

The apartment on the left?

This building is fucking huge. They can't live on half the fucking floor.

The elevator door opens on the third floor, and I am immediately proven wrong. There are only two apartments: A and B.

Apparently, fucking sugar daddies pays a lot better than I had originally thought.

The door to the apartment opens as I approach. Expecting to find either Nikki or Harper, I am taken off-guard by Edmund Parker almost bumping into me as he exits the apartment.

"Hmph, Detective Michales." He steps out of my way. "Funny running into you here. Are you related to Nikki?"

"Um, yeah," I lie.

"I'd love to catch up"— he's a facetious ass—"but I need to get back to Adelaide Cove."

Stepping into the apartment, I shut the door the door and am both relieved and disappointed to find both of the girls sitting on the couch.

Had they been dead, I might have finally been able to pin something on him.

"What the fuck was Edmund Parker doing here?" I stand over them.

"He stopped by asking to see me again," Harper answers.

"And what did you say?"

"I told him I'd have to think about it." My years of police work fail me, and I can't quite tell if she is being truthful.

"Did you fuck him?" The question escapes me without thinking. It has nothing to do with this case, my interest is sheerly out of jealousy.

"No." She shakes her head. "I mean, yes. But only that night on the video."

"How did the two of you wind up there that night?"

"Friend of a friend. Sort of," Nikki responds. "We'd heard rumblings about a party happening in Adelaide Cove from some girl at a bar downtown. She was drunk and gave us the info. We figured, what the hell."

"One thing led to another," Harper interjects. "And we wound up...well...you know."

"It's not the first time we've been to a party and wound up fucking the same guy," Nikki adds.

"You both really expect me to believe that?" I scoff.

Gripping Harper's face, I pull her from the couch and force her to look at me, "You're going to say yes to him. Eagerly yes to everything he asks of you. And every week when I come by, you're going to tell me everything you've learned about him and the fucking rich assholes he associates with."

She stares at me quietly.

"The more useful information you provide me." I grip her shoulder and press her toward the floor. "The less payment I'll require to keep your sweet, old nana from finding out what a dirty, fucking whore you are."

Knowing her role, Harper unzips my pants and pulls out my cock.

This isn't what I came here for...

Like her friend the other night, she swallows me with finesse.

...but I need the leverage and a reason to keep coming back.

"You too." I curl my finger at Nikki at she kneels on the floor beside her friend. The two of them slide their mouths along the sides of my shaft, playing with my balls, and they occasionally take turns swallowing me deep.

They're both too fucking good at this.

And I can't fight the urge to know why their tight little cunts are worth so much fucking money.

"Enough." They immediately follow my demand. Stepping away from them, I kick off my shoes while pulling my shirt over my head. After pushing off my pants, I take a seat in the chair beside the couch, my fist lightly gliding over the saliva they left on my cock.

"Clothes off." They both stare at me as they strip bare. The power I feel in this moment, it's as though there is nothing I couldn't ask of them.

It's a fucking trip.

Nikki takes a step toward me and stills when I shake my head.

"We have plenty of time. You're going to fuck each other first."

CHAPTER FORTY-NINE

ABIGAIL

Standing before the sink, finishing the last of curling my hair, I turn to find Grant standing in the doorway. In his hands are a bottle of lube and a plug—a very large, black plug.

"Lift your dress and bend over for me." He squeezes a generous amount of lube onto the plug before settling behind me. Using a firm hand to grip my ass, he slightly spreads my cheeks. He presses the tip into me, twisting and turning, before taking his time to work the remainder into me. Placing a kiss on my cheek, he lowers my dress and stands.

After washing his hands, he leans against the doorframe as he waits for me. He pulls his phone from his pocket and taps at the screen. The plug inside me vibrates, and my legs nearly crumple beneath me from the foreign sensation.

"Fuck, sir," I groan as he stops the buzzing.

He did say he's determined to ensure I enjoy this evening.

"I have one more surprise for this evening once you're ready."

"I'm ready, sir."

Grant retrieves a large, black leather jewelry box from the closet—the one we got the night of my collar. He opens the box and reveals a long, thick, platinum, chain. A thick, black leather loop for a handle at one end and a clasping hook at the other—a leash to go with my collar.

"It's beautiful." My fingers run along the clasp now hooked through my collar down to the leather in Grant's hand.

"You're the perfect fucking pet, kitten." He tugs the chain to pull me to him before kissing me deeply. "You fucking deserve it."

On the car ride to the estate, Grant asks me no less than ten times if I am excited for tonight.

Which I am, in a fueled with nerves kind of way.

I can't quite tell if he's giving me the opportunity to bow out or sharing how excited he is.

Pulling through the gates, my nerves begin to get the better of me. But when we pull into the clearing and I see the estate, my nerves quickly turn to dread. My thoughts flood with the disgust on his face as he shared me with Will. My heart physically hurts remembering the pain I felt that night.

"We don't have to do this." The words blubber from my mouth. "I don't want you to share me with Will, Edmund, or Samuel if it's going to end like it did last time."

"Kitten, I have no intentions of letting any of them so much as lay a finger on you, much less put their cocks inside of you."

"But..." Confusion wafts over me he helps me from the car an into the house. Walking through the door, Liz is coming down the last of the stairs.

"Perfect timing," she addresses Grant. "I just left your entertainment upstairs. I gave you the Alaskan King, so you have plenty of room for everyone."

"This is fucking gorgeous." Her hand dusts over his, and slides along the chain to the loop at my throat. Hooking her finger into it, she places a soft, wet kiss on my lips, and I am quickly reminded how much I enjoyed her lips and delicate tongue when she kissed me previously.

"You're a lucky fucking pet." Her lips buzz against mine. "And I'd be lying if I didn't say I were a tiny bit jealous of what he's giving you."

Keeping the slack of the chain short, Grant pulls me up the stairs behind him. He opens the bedroom door and I'm surprised to find two beautiful women in lingerie laying on the bed.

"There is no way in hell I'm letting another man fuck you, kitten." His words are deep and sincere. "I'm fulfilling your fantasy the way I can. They are fully prepared fill your cunt and mouth like you want."

Grant pulls me into the room, and closes the door and locks it to give us privacy. Unclipping my leash and removing my dress, he addresses the women on the bed.

"You are here for her. Your job is to please her and fulfill her desires. Do you understand?"

Both women nod in agreement as their eyes roam over my body, leaving me feeling so fucking wanted.

"I have a handful of unwavering rules: Do not mark her. Her perfect fucking peach of an ass is off-limits. Tonight is not about your pleasure. And when I decide to join you, neither of you lay a hand on me without her permission."

My head snaps around to Grant, the significance of his final rule not lost on me. Ignoring my reaction, he takes a seat in a chair at the foot of the bed.

Delicate hands roam from my shoulder to my hand, as the blonde slides her fingers into mine and gingerly leads me to the bed as she reassures me, "No need to be nervous, sweetie. You're in charge, and we're going to give you everything you want."

The two of them kneel on the bed next to me. Their soft hands roam over every inch of my skin as they kiss every place they touch. The brunette softly slips her tongue into my mouth, gently playing with mine, and the blonde positions herself behind me. She continues to place wet kisses on my neck as the brunette begins making her way down my stomach.

Her hand softly rubs over the wet lace of my panties. I twitch in response, and she continues to kiss her way to the top of my panties. The blonde I'm resting against gently kneads at my breasts as she reassures me, "Relax, sweetie. Enjoy this gift your sir has given you."

CHAPTER FIFTY

GRANT

Abigail's eyes lock on mine when directed by the experienced switch behind her, who was hand-picked to ensure my kitten was relaxed and enjoying the experience —providing soft dominance as needed.

She's earning every fucking penny.

"Spread those thighs, sweetie." The blonde continues to provide direction that Abigail follows perfectly. "Eyes on your sir as you enjoy the feel of her tongue sliding over your clit. Watch how much he enjoys seeing you like this."

The brunette between Abigail's thighs pulls the lace of her panties to the side and licks her from the entrance to clit, and Abigail moans in response. Her moans travel straight to my cock.

"I love your fucking moans, kitten." I palm over my cock. "Let us all hear how much you enjoy her eating your sweet cunt."

Hooking an arm under Abigail's knee, the blonde spreads her wide and holds her open as the brunette licks and sucks at her swollen clit. Her tits are pulled from her bra, and the blonde behind her toys with her nipples. The two of them causing Abigail to fill the room with mewls.

"Are they going to make you come, kitten?" I question while fighting the urge to join them and push her over the edge. "Come for them."

"Your sir wants you to come. Are you going to disobey him?" the blonde whispers in her ear while continuing to play with her nipples. Abigail's back arches and she cries out as they bring her over the edge.

"Another," I demand, flipping the anal vibe to the lowest setting before I begin removing my clothes. Without hesitation, they both follow my demands.

Abigail's eyes follow me as I walk to the side of the bed. Bending down, I claim her mouth and swallow her screams as the firm licks of her clit and vibrations in her ass do her in.

"You taste so fucking good, baby," The brunette places scattered kisses on Abigail's stomach before kissing the blonde deeply.

"Fuck, she is delicious," the blonde groans as I drag Abigail onto my lap. "I want to bury my face in her as you fuck her."

Sliding into Abigail, I lean back on the headboard and pull her backward with me. Her back is on my chest and her legs straddle my thighs, the blonde eagerly licks at her available clit.

"You're so fucking wet." I thrust up into her hard and deep. "And you're shaking, kitten."

"It's so much." The words tremble over her lips.

"It's going to be so much more. You've still got two more cocks to go." I look to the foot of the bed to find the brunette ready.

"Come on my cock, kitten. And then you can come on hers." I nip at the side of her neck and pull her attention to the brunette adorning a more than adequately sized strap-on.

Quivering on my lap, Abigail claws at my thighs as she comes again. Sliding Abigail off my cock, the blonde wipes arousal from her face before helping me slide her over the silicone cock.

"Ride that fucking cock for me," I slap her ass. "Show me how eager you are to have mine in your mouth."

Struggling through her exhaustion, she undulates her hips and grinds over the strap-on. The woman beneath her grips her hips, helping her to set a steady pace. Heavy breaths and moans begin to fill the room as they find her rhythm.

Standing on the bed, I straddle the brunette and grip the hair at the nape of Abigail's neck. Gripping my shaft with the other, I press it to her lips. Looking up at me through her lashes, her gaze is filled with lust.

I hold her head steady as I slide into her mouth and down her throat. "I want you to come on her cock while I fuck your pretty little mouth. I'm not stopping until you're screaming around my cock."

Clutching her head with my other hand, I give a few shallow thrusts into her mouth before burying myself deep in her throat. Abigail holds her lips to the base of my shaft as she continues to grind her hips, climbing higher toward her next orgasm.

Repeating the shallow thrusts, I give her a moment to catch her breath before pushing all the way into her again. This time I don't still. I thrust hard and deep, thoroughly enjoying the watering of her eyes and her gags causing her throat to constrict tightly around my cock.

Tears rolls down her cheeks, and when her eyes meet mine, it almost does me in. Pulling back, I attempt to give myself some reprieve. Instead, Abigail sucks at me diligently, the moans of her orgasm vibrating around my cock.

"Fuck, kitten." I pull myself from her mouth. "Keep sucking like that and I won't be able to fill your ass."

Kneeling beside her, I take her face in my hands. Possessively, I pull her close and kiss her hard and deep, swallowing the whimpers that vibrate through my mouth. Both of us are near breathless when I pull back and break our kiss.

"You're doing so fucking good." I place a soft kiss on her forehead as I move out of the way to make room for the blonde who's about to take my spot. "My perfect little pet deserves every fucking minute of this.

CHAPTER FIFTY-ONE

ABIGAIL

From now on, it's probably a good idea to be careful what you wish for Abigail.

This is as an enjoyable and painful as when Grant strapped the fucking wand to my thigh. Each orgasm a sheer moment of bliss before painfully building up to another few seconds of release.

The blonde kneels at the shoulders of the brunette beneath me. Sliding her fingers into my hair, she is gentle. Gripping the shaft of the silicone dick strapped to her hips, she drips a mouthful of her spit onto the head. It begins to run down the shaft as she drags my lips to the tip.

"You set the pace, sweetie." She presses it between my lips as she strokes my face.

The bed shifts, and Grant settles behind me. His hand slides up my back as he bends me over further, allowing him to pull the vibrating plug from my ass.

He aligns with my stretched hole, and I immediately tense. Both women still, their hands reassuringly rubbing over my body.

Suddenly terrified.

Afraid I can't take it all.

"Relax, kitten." Grant rubs his tip around my hole, "You know you can take my cock in your ass. You fucking love how I fill this tight little hole, don't you?"

"Yes, sir," I groan as he presses the head inside me.

"That's it. Relax for me." He continues to press inside me an inch a time, "Keep letting me in."

He bottoms out inside me, sucking in a breath, he grunts, "Fuck! You're so fucking tight with her cock in your cunt."

Grant slowly moves his hips, and I can't help the groan the billows from my lungs.

It feels like they're going to fucking split me in two.

"You can do this," the brunette encourages me. "Let us do the work."

She takes up the same slow pace as Grant, the two of them pulling from and thrusting into me in tandem.

"Yes." the word falls out of my mouth as the pleasure they are providing replaces the painful stretch of being so full.

"I need more, kitten," Grant moans from behind me as his fingers dig into the meaty flesh of my ass. "I need you to take my fucking cock in your ass like the good little whore you are."

He slides into me a little harder, and I push back, inadvertently sliding myself over the cock in my pussy, wanting him to do it again.

"Fuck me," I groan.

"Good fucking girl." Grant and the brunette both begin to increase their pace. "I want you screaming around that cock as you come until I fill this tight fucking hole with cum. Understood?"

"Yes, sir." The breathy words shake from me as the blonde presses back into my mouth. She fucks my mouth shallow and gentle, while Grant and the brunette fuck me at a savage pace.

They feel so fucking good.

Filling me to the brink.

"I'm going to fucking come," I scream the words from the build-up as they force me over the edge. An orgasm like nothing I have ever experienced before shoots through every nerve and ripples through my body. And I scream through the waves of my repeated release.

Every muscle in my body twitches as the two of them continue their unrelenting rhythm. The overload of pleasure is too much for my body to handle.

"You're shaking so fucking hard, kitten. You're going to fucking force me to come."

"Please," I beg.

Grant plunges deep into my ass, and he twitches inside me as his cum fills me. His hips flex against my ass, and the blonde climbs from the bed. His sputtering stills, and he carefully pulls himself from me.

"You did amazing for your first time." The brunette smiles at me as Grant rolls me off her body. "You should be fucking proud of yourself."

The moment she is no longer inside of me, she climbs from the bed and disappears from the room.

"I'm so fucking proud of you, kitten." Grant holds me tight to his body. He brushes the sweaty hair from my face to kiss my lips.

His lips linger against mine long after our kiss.

"Thank you, sir." My breaths are still heavy. "For tonight. For indulging my fantasy."

"I meant it earlier, kitten. You deserve every bit of tonight."

"For being such a good pet?"

"No." He presses his lips to my forehead. "For being the most perfect thing in my life."

.

EPILOGUE

GRANT

ONE MONTH LATER

We've been managing to keep things at bay with Detective Michales, with Nikki and Harper taking the brunt of the burden. At the rate we're paying them to keep him occupied, they'll both be able to retire for life by the end of next year.

Edmund put a crinkle in our plan when he decided to start fucking Harper, and I still can't fathom the fact that he is knowingly sticking his cock in the same hole as that fucking pig.

Liz, Abigail, and I think we finally figured out a way to use that convoluted love triangle to our advantage.

Actually, it was mostly Abigail.

I believe her now.

All those times she told me she wasn't looking for me to change, to be a good man for her. With every day that passes, I feel as though she bends more toward my morality than I do toward hers.

She might be the most innocent of us, but she has no issues walking hand in hand with the devil. A side of her the others are quickly becoming more familiar with as she continues to embrace the depraved things the world has to offer.

A side of her I'm fucking feral for.

———

"You've been glued to that phone all morning, kitten."

"The gallery in The Village wants more paintings," she excitedly responds. "They can't seem to keep them on the walls."

"Speaking of which. If you ever get off that phone, I have something in the other room for you."

She follows eagerly behind me and gasps at the painting hanging on the wall in her conservatory.

"You didn't!" she squeals. "How? When?"

"I did," I mock her. "I've been fighting with Nikolai over the price since the night I realized how much you loved it, how badly you wanted it. Based on how steadfast he was, I'm quite certain he knew as well. We finally agreed the other night, and I had it picked up this morning."

"Are you getting all romantic and sentimental on me?" She turns to face me, and I'm met with a sheepish smirk.

"Not in the slightest, kitten." I bend down to grip her thighs and pull them around my waist. Her short skirt rides over her ass as I drive her into the wall beside the painting. Two fucking masterpieces side by side.

Fumbling beneath her to free my cock, I drive it into her. I fuck her hard, sliding her back against the wall with each thrust. The opportunity to savor her can happen later. Now, I want to hear her scream as she comes around my cock.

The best fucking thank you she can give me.

Both of us spent, we crumple to a heap together on the floor with my cock still buried inside her.

The doorbell rings interrupting our moment of bliss.

"I'll get it." Abigail climbs from my lap and shimmies her skirt back down her thighs.

It rings again. Someone is incessantly pressing the button outside.

"I'm coming," Abigail shouts from the foyer as I finish tucking myself into my pants to follow after her.

"Grant!" Abigail's voice sounds frightened.

Stepping into the foyer, I see Samuel. His clothes are soaked in blood—too much to be his own—and splatters speckle his skin. Except for his hands, which are stained as red as his clothes.

His eyes meet mine and he says, "I fucked up..."

THANK YOU FOR READING

I hope you enjoyed the beginning of the Grant and Abigail's story!

If you did, the best support you can give to an indie author, like myself, is to tell others about my book. Reviews left on Goodreads, Amazon, or anywhere else you are comfortable truly mean the world to me.

Want to know what happens next in Adelaide Cove? Check out the series!

ALSO BY J.L. QUICK

THE MEN OF CLUB TRISKELION SERIES

- Owned
- Bound
- Primal
- Master (Coming Spring 2025)
- Shared (Coming Spring 2025)
- Daddy (Coming Spring 2025)

THE BOTTICELLI BROTHERHOOD SERIES

- Sold to the Syndicate
- Capo Dei Capi's Daughter
- Indebted to the Enemy
- Falling for the Mafia Dom

THE MARCANO MOGULS SERIES

- Tryst
- Crave
- Intern
- Savage